Legends

Volume 1

Thomas W. Campbell

About Legends Volume 1

This book is intended to honor the legacy and wisdom of these extraordinary individuals while providing readers with thought-provoking perspectives on timeless themes of success, leadership, and human achievement.

This is a fictional work. Apart from the person referred to as the Legend, all other names, characters, locations, and events are either products of the author's imagination or used in a fictitious manner. Any similarity to real individuals, whether living or deceased, actual events, or real places is purely coincidental.

The stories and conversations presented in Legends Volume 1 were created for inspirational and educational purposes. While the biographical information, historical details, and life events of each figure are based on widely documented facts and common knowledge, the specific advice, dialogue, and personal reflections attributed to these individuals are entirely fictional and represent the author's interpretation of what these remarkable people might say based on their known philosophies, writings, and documented beliefs.

Any quotes or statements not explicitly cited from historical records should be understood as creative interpretations rather than actual words spoken or written by these figures. Readers are encouraged to explore the actual writings, speeches, and documented works of these legends to gain deeper insight into their authentic voices and teachings.

Publisher Information

Legends, Volume 1
First Edition: October 1, 2025
ISBN
979-8-218-81581-3
979-8-218-82284-2

Published by

Sherlock Holmes Society USA
P. O. Box 347
Carolina Beach, NC   28428

Contact

Thomas W. Campbell
SHolmesSociety@gmail.com

Printed in the United States of America

Identity Chart

The front cover art of Legends Volume 1 features twenty extraordinary individuals whose lives and achievements have fundamentally shaped human civilization.

Each legend represents a different pathway to greatness, ensuring that readers encounter diverse perspectives on leadership, creativity, perseverance, and purpose. Together, they form a comprehensive guide to the qualities and insights that define truly transformational lives.

The following reference chart corresponds to the front cover layout, allowing you to easily identify each legend featured in this volume.

Abraham Lincoln	Steve Jobs	Martin Luther King	John Fitzgerald Kennedy	Lucille Ball
Walter Cronkite	Sir Arthur Conan Doyle	Marilyn Monroe	Margaret Thatcher	Jackie Robinson
Admiral Chester Nimitz	Thomas Jefferson	Amelia Earhart	Albert Einstein	Mahatma Ghandi
John Coltrane	Howard Hughes	Henry Ford	John Wayne	Arthur Miller

Introduction

In this captivating collection of stories, history's most influential figures step from the pages of the past to offer their hard-earned wisdom for today's world. Legends Volume 1 presents a glimpse into the remarkable lives of 20 visionaries, innovators, leaders, and trailblazers.

Through carefully crafted fictional dialogues grounded in historical truth, these legends reveal the principles, perspectives, and philosophies that guided their ground-breaking achievements.

From overcoming seemingly impossible obstacles to revolutionizing entire fields of human endeavor, these remarkable figures offer practical advice on leadership, creativity, perseverance, and finding purpose in an ever-changing world.

Legends Volume 1 bridges the gap between past and present, transforming historical biography into a personal mentorship experience. Readers will discover not just what these great minds accomplished, but how they thought, what drove them, and what wisdom they would impart to help others navigate the challenges and opportunities of modern life.

As the title suggests, this book represents the first Volume of an ongoing series. Our world contains countless legends whose wisdom deserves to be heard, and additional volumes will be published in the near future to share more of their invaluable insights!

Table of Contents

President Abraham Lincoln

Abraham Lincoln was the 16th President of the United States who led the nation through the Civil War, preserved the Union, issued the Emancipation Proclamation to free enslaved people, and delivered iconic speeches like the Gettysburg Address before being assassinated in 1865, making him one of America's greatest presidents and a martyr for freedom and unity.

The Prairie Lawyer

The study on the University of Georgia campus was lined with books about American history, and afternoon sunlight filtered through tall windows that offered a view of the historic North Campus quad. Matt sat across from Amy in her office at the History Department, speaking with one of the nation's foremost Lincoln scholars. Amy had spent decades studying not just Lincoln's public life, but his private correspondence, his relationships with family and friends, and the psychological dimensions of his leadership during America's darkest hour.

"Amy," Matt began, adjusting his recording device in the professor's book-lined office, "I want to ask you to engage in a thought experiment. It's April 13th, 1865. The war is essentially over—Lee surrendered just four days earlier. If someone had approached Lincoln that day and asked him to share his most important advice for living a good life, what do you think he would have said?"

Amy leaned back in her chair, her eyes thoughtful as she gazed momentarily toward the window overlooking the tree-lined campus. "That's a fascinating question, Matt, especially given what we know was about to happen. I think Lincoln's advice would have been deeply shaped by his recent experiences—not just the war, but his profound personal losses."

"What do you mean specifically?"

"Well, by April 1865, Lincoln had lived through an extraordinary series of failures and setbacks. His early business ventures failed so completely that friends called his debts 'the National Debt.' He lost multiple elections—the Illinois legislature in 1832, Speaker of the House, Congress in 1843, the Senate twice. But I think he would have framed these not as defeats, but as essential education."

Matt nodded, noting the afternoon light streaming across the professor's desk. "So his advice would focus on failure?"

"I think he would have said something like: 'Let your failures teach you what your successes cannot.' Lincoln seemed to extract wisdom from every setback. After losing to Stephen Douglas in 1858, he didn't retreat—he used those debates to refine his arguments against slavery and build his national reputation. I believe he would have told people that failure isn't the opposite of success, but rather its teacher."

"That's interesting. What else do you think would have been on his mind that day?"

Amy paused, considering, her gaze moving across the volumes of American history that filled her office. "Education, absolutely. Here was a man born to illiterate parents in a one-room log cabin, who became one of America's most eloquent writers and speakers through sheer determination to learn. His stepmother Sarah Bush Lincoln brought a Bible, Aesop's

Fables, and Pilgrim's Progress into their home, and Lincoln read them by firelight until he'd memorized whole passages."

"And his advice about education would be what?"

"I imagine something like: 'Never allow your circumstances to define the boundaries of your mind.' Lincoln proved that a person with access to books and the will to learn them could compete intellectually with anyone, regardless of their station. Education wasn't something that happened to him—it was something he seized for himself, day after day, year after year."

Matt leaned forward in his chair, the sounds of campus life barely audible through the windows. "You mentioned his personal losses. How do you think those would have influenced his advice?"

Amy's expression grew more somber. "By April 1865, Lincoln had buried two children—Eddie in 1850 from consumption, and Willie in 1862 from fever, right there in the White House. He'd watched Mary struggle with grief and mental illness. He'd carried the weight of 600,000 war deaths on his conscience. I think those experiences would have made his advice deeply personal."

"In what way?"

"I believe he would have warned about the cost of duty. Lincoln understood that serving something greater than yourself is noble and necessary, but he also lived with the regret of time lost with his family. There's evidence he felt he'd missed too many precious moments with his children because of the demands of politics and governance."

Matt nodded. "So what would he have said about balancing public duty and private life?"

"Something like: 'No cause, however noble, should rob you entirely of the simple joys that make life meaningful.' Or perhaps: 'We serve the future, but we must not forget to live in the present.' Lincoln would sit with Tad on his lap while working, let Willie interrupt important meetings. He understood instinctively that the private man serves those he loves, and that duty is as sacred as public service."

"That's quite poignant, given the timing," Matt observed, glancing around the scholarly atmosphere of Amy's office.

"Exactly. And I think Lincoln would also have emphasized the importance of surrounding yourself with people who challenge you. His Cabinet strategy was revolutionary—he appointed his rivals for the Republican nomination: Seward, Chase, Bates. Most politicians want yes-men, but Lincoln actively sought out those who would disagree with him."

"What advice would that translate to?"

"I think he would have said: 'Seek out those who will tell you uncomfortable truths, because comfortable lies will lead you to disaster.' Lincoln understood that isolation breeds poor judgment. A leader who hears only agreement will soon find himself agreeing with catastrophe."

Matt made a note, appreciating the quiet scholarly environment that seemed perfect for this kind of deep historical reflection. "You've studied his decision-making process extensively. What else might he have shared about leadership?"

"The importance of timing. Lincoln held the Emancipation Proclamation in his desk drawer for months, waiting for the right moment—after a Union victory at Antietam. He wasn't hesitating because he doubted its necessity, but because he understood that timing in matters of great import can mean the difference between success and catastrophe."

"So his advice would be?"

"Something like: 'Sometimes a leader must act on incomplete information, but other times patience is more important than speed. Wisdom lies in knowing the difference.' Lincoln understood that good intentions without strategic thinking often backfire."

Matt shifted in his chair. "What about his famous storytelling ability? How do you think that would have factored into his advice?"

Amy smiled, her enthusiasm for the subject evident in her office surrounded by decades of Lincoln research. "Oh, absolutely central. Lincoln believed you could change minds through stories better than through arguments. He was always using anecdotes to make his points, even during Cabinet meetings. I think he would have advised: 'A well-chosen story is worth a dozen logical proofs. People remember what moves them, not what merely convinces them.'"

"And his humor? Even during the darkest moments of the war, he seemed to find ways to lighten the mood."

"That's right. I think Lincoln would have said something like: 'Cultivate the ability to find light moments even in dark times.' His humor wasn't just personal therapy—it was a leadership tool. It helped him connect with people and defuse tension when emotions ran too high for productive discussion."

Matt paused thoughtfully, the late afternoon Georgia sun casting long shadows across the campus visible from the professor's window. "Amy, given everything you've said, do you think Lincoln would have been satisfied with how his life turned out, if he'd had that moment of reflection on April 13th?"

Amy considered this carefully from her position behind the desk that had served her through decades of teaching and research. "That's profound, Matt. I think he would have felt the weight of what he'd accomplished—preserving the Union, beginning the end of slavery—but also the profound personal costs. Lincoln was never entirely comfortable with praise, and he understood better than most that even great achievements come with unintended consequences."

"So his final piece of advice might have been what?"

"I believe he would have returned to that theme of integration—balancing the grand and the intimate. Perhaps something like: 'History may judge your public actions, but you must live with your private choices. Both matter. The public man serves the nation, but the private man serves those he loves, and both duties are sacred.'"

Matt set down his pen, the quietude of the campus adding gravity to the moment. "There's something especially moving about imagining him offering this wisdom less than 24 hours before John Wilkes Booth would end his life at Ford's Theatre."

"Yes," Amy agreed quietly from her office overlooking the historic grounds. "Whether Lincoln had any premonition or not, there's something about his character that suggests he understood how quickly everything could change. He'd lived through so much loss and uncertainty. I think that would have made his advice feel urgent—not abstract or preachy, but the kind of hard-won wisdom someone shares when they understand how precious and finite time really is."

"And perhaps that sense of time's fragility would have made him especially focused on what truly matters?"

"Exactly. At the end of the day, Lincoln was a prairie lawyer who happened to find himself at the center of the greatest crisis in American history. But underneath all the grand historical narrative, he remained someone who understood the value of simple human connections—reading stories to your children, sharing a joke with a friend, taking time to really listen when someone needs to be heard."

Matt looked at his notes, filled with insights about failure as teacher, education as self-liberation, the costs of duty, the importance of dissenting voices, the power of timing and storytelling. "Amy, it strikes me that the advice you've imagined isn't just about leadership or politics, but about living with integrity."

"That's exactly right, Matt. Lincoln's greatness wasn't just in what he accomplished, but in how he remained fundamentally human while carrying inhuman burdens. His hypothetical final advice would have been about how to do that—how to serve something larger than yourself without losing yourself in the process."

As the interview concluded in the peaceful setting of the History Department, Matt reflected on how Amy had woven together the public and private Lincoln—the self-made man and the grieving father, the strategic politician and the compassionate friend. In imagining Lincoln's final wisdom within the scholarly atmosphere of the campus, she had captured something essential about his enduring appeal: he was great not in spite of his humanity, but because of it.

Steve Jobs

Steve Jobs was the visionary co-founder and CEO of Apple who revolutionized technology and multiple industries through iconic products like the iPhone, iPad, and iPod, becoming synonymous with innovative design, perfectionism, and the intersection of technology and liberal arts.

Stay Hungry, Stay Human

The late afternoon sun filtered through the tall windows of MIT's Student Center, casting long shadows across the nearly empty study area. Aaron sat hunched over his laptop, but his screen had long since gone dark. His friend Laura noticed his distant expression as she approached with two steaming cups of coffee.

"You're doing that thing again," Laura said, setting a cup in front of him and settling into the chair across the small table. "That faraway look you get when you're thinking about your tech heroes."

Aaron smiled sheepishly and accepted the coffee gratefully. "Steve Jobs, actually. I've been wondering what he might say to our generation if he could. You know, what final wisdom he'd want to leave behind."

Laura raised an eyebrow. Coming from anyone else, this might have seemed like idle speculation, but she knew Aaron had spent countless hours studying not just Apple's products, but Jobs himself—his philosophy, his evolution as a leader, his approach to innovation. The Think Different poster above Aaron's desk wasn't just decoration; it represented a genuine fascination with how great minds approached impossible problems.

"I keep thinking about this idea of following curiosity instead of crowds," Aaron continued, warming to his subject. "When Jobs and Wozniak started Apple, everyone thought they were crazy. The computer industry belonged to IBM. But they saw something different—they saw that technology should serve humanity, not the other way around."

Laura nodded, understanding where this was heading. She'd heard Aaron articulate similar thoughts before, usually when they were working late on particularly challenging projects. "Like how they made computers personal instead of just powerful."

"Exactly. And that came from genuine curiosity about what was possible, not from market research telling them what to build." Aaron took a sip of his coffee, organizing his thoughts. "But here's what I find most interesting about Jobs—I think by the end, he understood that his greatest insights weren't just about products. They were about people."

This caught Laura's attention. It wasn't the angle she expected from Aaron, who usually focused on the technical brilliance of Apple's designs.

Aaron continued, his voice taking on a more reflective tone. "I've been reading about how he evolved as a leader. Early on, he was notorious for being brutal in his pursuit of perfection. He'd tear apart designs that would have made Apple millions because they weren't magical enough. Every pixel mattered. Every curve. Every click."

"That sounds like the Steve Jobs everyone knows," Laura said.

"Right, but here's the thing—I think he realized later that you could demand excellence without destroying the people around you. That some of the most talented people left Apple not because they couldn't meet his standards, but because they couldn't endure how those standards were communicated."

Laura leaned forward, intrigued by this perspective. "You're saying he learned to separate the pursuit of perfection from personal cruelty?"

"I think so. Excellence and empathy aren't opposites—they're partners." Aaron paused, considering his words carefully. "The best engineering teams I've worked with here at MIT aren't the ones where everyone's afraid to speak up. They're the ones where people feel safe to fail fast, iterate, and push boundaries."

The campus around them was quieting as evening approached, but their conversation was just gaining momentum. Laura found herself thinking about their current projects, about the difference between constructive feedback and destructive criticism.

"There's something else too," Aaron said. "Jobs talked a lot about simplicity, but I think he understood it as more than just design philosophy. Anyone can make something complicated. Real genius is making something simple. The iPod succeeded not because it did more than other MP3 players, but because it did less—better."

"A thousand songs in your pocket," Laura quoted.

"Simple. Magical. Revolutionary," Aaron finished. "But I think he applied that same principle to life itself. Focus on what matters. Say no to a thousand good ideas so you can say yes to the few great ones."

Laura considered this, thinking about her own tendency to overcommit to projects and opportunities. "That's actually profound advice for anyone at MIT. We're constantly bombarded with amazing opportunities."

"And here's another thing—Jobs insisted on building products he'd want to use himself. The iPhone wasn't created because market research demanded it. It was created because they wanted a phone that was also an iPod, a camera, an internet device. Something that had never existed but should have."

Aaron's eyes lit up as he connected these ideas. "Design isn't just how something looks—it's how it works. Beauty without function is just decoration. Function without beauty is just engineering. Magic happens when both come together seamlessly."

"You're talking about more than product design now, aren't you?" Laura asked.

"I think Jobs would say you should design your life, your relationships, your legacy with the same care you'd design a product you're proud to put your name on." Aaron paused, struck by the weight of his own words. "Leave something behind that wasn't there before. Make a dent in the universe."

The phrase hung in the air between them. Around the nearly empty student center, a few other students were packing up their belongings, preparing to head back to their dorms or labs. The familiar rhythm of MIT campus life continued, but Aaron and Laura found themselves caught in a moment of deeper reflection.

"You know what I think his final message would be?" Aaron asked, his voice quieter now. "Stay hungry, stay foolish—but also stay human. Don't get so caught up in the pursuit of excellence that you forget the people around you are human beings with hopes and fears and feelings just as real as your own."

Laura smiled at this evolution of the famous quote. "So his ultimate wisdom wasn't just about innovation or business success."

"No, I think it was about learning that knowing your time is limited clarifies what's worth doing and what isn't. Strip away everything that doesn't matter, and what remains is what you'll be remembered for." Aaron looked out at the campus, where the first lights were beginning to flicker on in the gathering dusk.

"Behind every employee badge, every team member, every collaborator, there's a human being who chose to work alongside you, who committed their talent to a shared vision. The real legacy isn't just the products you create—it's the example of how you treat people while creating them."

Laura sat back in her chair, processing this perspective on someone she'd always thought of primarily as a tech visionary. "That's beautiful, actually. Here's a guy who revolutionized how humans interact with technology, and his ultimate advice is about preserving our humanity."

Aaron nodded, feeling like he'd finally articulated something he'd been grappling with for months. "Maybe that's why he remains such a compelling figure. He showed that even the most driven, perfectionist leaders can evolve. They can learn to lead with both excellence and empathy."

As the evening settled over MIT, both friends sat quietly for a moment, each contemplating the kind of technologists they wanted to become. The conversation had started as speculation about a hero's final wisdom, but it had become something more—a reflection on their own values and aspirations.

"To making a dent in the universe," Laura said finally, raising her coffee cup in a mock toast.

"The right way," Aaron replied, meeting her gesture.

Outside the windows, the campus buzzed with the quiet energy of brilliant minds at work, each pursuing their own vision of what technology could accomplish. But in that moment, Aaron felt he understood something essential about the intersection of ambition and humanity—a lesson that would shape not just his career, but his character.

Dr. Martin Luther King, Jr.

Martin Luther King Jr. was a Baptist minister and civil rights leader who championed nonviolent resistance to fight racial segregation and inequality, delivering his iconic "I Have a Dream" speech during the 1963 March on Washington and leading pivotal movements like the Montgomery Bus Boycott before being assassinated in 1968, becoming a symbol of the struggle for racial justice and equality in America.

Echoes in the Sanctuary

The afternoon light filtered through the stained glass windows of Atlanta's Ebenezer Baptist Church, casting colorful patterns across the worn wooden pews. Pastor Mike sat in the front row with Mrs. Ruby Thiel, whose weathered hands held decades of stories. At eighty-four, she was one of the few remaining congregants who remembered when Dr. King's voice had filled this very sanctuary.

"Pastor, you asked me last week about what Dr. King might say to us today," Mrs. Thiel began, her voice carrying the weight of memory. "I've been thinking about that ever since."

Pastor Mike leaned forward, sensing the gravity in her tone. "You knew him personally, didn't you, Mrs. Thiel?"

"I was sixteen when I first met him, right here after a Sunday service in 1963. My grandmother introduced me---said I was going to be somebody important one day." She chuckled softly. "I was just a scared teenager, but Dr. King had this way of making you feel like your voice mattered."

"What do you remember most about him?"

"His eyes," she said without hesitation. "They held so much---pain, yes, but also this unshakeable hope. Even when things looked darkest, he never stopped believing change was possible. He used to tell us young folks, 'Don't underestimate the power of ordinary people united by an extraordinary cause.'"

Pastor Mike nodded. "We could use that reminder today. Sometimes our congregation feels so small against all the problems we're facing."

Mrs. Thiel's expression grew thoughtful. "Dr. King would say that's exactly the wrong way to think about it. He'd remind us that fifty thousand people sustained the Montgomery Bus Boycott for over a year---381 days!---just by walking. Walking, Pastor. Nothing fancy, just putting one foot in front of the other because they believed right would prevail."

"But the challenges today feel different, don't they? The divisions seem deeper, the anger more raw."

"Oh, child," Mrs. Thiel shook her head, "Dr. King faced dogs and fire hoses. He got beaten bloody on bridges. The temptation toward violence was enormous---I remember the young men in our community who wanted to fight back with fists instead of prayers. But he always said the same thing: 'We must absorb hatred rather than return it.' Not because it was easy, but because only love could secure lasting peace."

Pastor Mike shifted in his seat. "Sometimes I wonder if that message of nonviolence still resonates. Young people today seem so frustrated with the pace of change."

"Dr. King understood that frustration better than anyone," Mrs. Thiel replied firmly. "He got criticized constantly---by white moderates who thought he was moving too fast, by younger activists who thought he was moving too slow. When he spoke out against the Vietnam War, even some of our closest allies abandoned the movement. They said he was overreaching."

"How did he handle that isolation?"

"He said moral leadership sometimes means standing alone, trusting that history will vindicate your conscience even when popular opinion condemns it. But he also taught us something else---expect to be misunderstood, even by those who should be your allies. The key is not to let that stop you from doing what's right."

Pastor Mike was quiet for a moment, then asked, "What about when people lose hope? When they look around and see the same injustices, the same inequalities, sometimes worse than before?"

Mrs. Thiel's voice grew stronger. "Dr. King would say that setbacks are just setups for comebacks. You know, the Albany campaign was considered a failure, but it taught the movement lessons that made Birmingham possible. When they criticized bringing children into the Birmingham demonstrations--- children as young as six---Dr. King knew it was a tremendous risk. But those young people showed courage that awakened the conscience of a nation."

"So you think he'd tell us to keep taking risks?"

"Bold risks, but smart ones. He believed in what he called 'creative tension'---the kind of pressure that forces a community to confront its contradictions. Progress isn't given freely by those in power; it must be demanded by those who lack it."

Pastor Mike leaned back, processing this. "Mrs. Thiel, what do you think Dr. King would say about the economic struggles our community faces today? The gentrification, the lack of opportunities?"

"Oh, Pastor, that would be at the center of everything he'd tell us today." Her eyes lit up with passion. "Dr. King learned that economic justice and racial justice are inseparable. Fighting for the right to vote means nothing if people lack the economic power to make their votes matter. He used to say 'poverty anywhere threatens prosperity everywhere.'"

"But how do we bridge those divides? It feels like we're more separated than ever---not just by race, but by class, by politics, by everything."

Mrs. Thiel smiled, the same smile she'd worn as a teenager when Dr. King had first taken her seriously. "He'd tell you the same thing he told us then: build bridges, not walls. Some of our greatest victories came from unexpected allies. Remember the March on Washington---a quarter million Americans of all races. The white clergymen who joined us in Selma. He showed us that the struggle for justice belongs to all humanity."

"That seems so hard to imagine right now, with all the anger and division."

"Dr. King would remind you that the ultimate goal isn't to defeat your enemies but to transform them into friends. After the buses were integrated in Montgomery, they didn't celebrate by humiliating those who had opposed them. They invited them to ride together as equals. That's the difference between a protest movement and a true revolution of values."

Pastor Mike stood and walked to the window, looking out at the Atlanta skyline. "Sometimes I feel the weight of following in his footsteps, trying to lead this congregation through these times."

"Pastor," Mrs. Thiel's voice was gentle but firm, "Dr. King would be the first to tell you that the movement is larger than any single leader. He insisted this struggle belonged to the people, not to Martin Luther King. Mrs. Parks, Ralph Abernathy, Diane Nash, John Lewis, Fannie Lou Hamer---and countless others whose names never made the history books. When leaders emerge, they must never forget they're servants of a cause much greater than themselves."

"So the pressure shouldn't all be on me?"

"The pressure should be on all of us. Dr. King would say the arc of the moral universe bends toward justice, but only because people are willing to grab hold of it and pull. Justice isn't inevitable---it requires the active participation of everyone who believes in it."

Pastor Mike returned to his seat, something shifting in his demeanor. "What about hope, Mrs. Thiel? In your darkest moments, how do you hold onto it?"

"The same way Dr. King did when our headquarters got bombed, when he was stabbed, when death threats became daily reality. Hope isn't optimism, child. It's a discipline. It's the decision to believe that love is stronger than hate, that truth is more powerful than lies, that justice will ultimately prevail."

The light in the church had shifted as they talked, the afternoon growing longer. Pastor Mike felt something he hadn't felt in months---not just hope, but clarity.

"Mrs. Thiel, if Dr. King were sitting here with us right now, what would be his final word?"

She was quiet for a long moment, her eyes distant. "He'd probably talk about balance. Near the end, I remember him struggling with how much the movement demanded of him---time away from his family, from his children. He'd want future leaders to find a way to serve the cause without sacrificing the relationships that give life its deepest meaning."

She reached over and patted Pastor Mike's hand. "But mostly, he'd remind us that each generation must take up the unfinished work of democracy. We have to continue the struggle to make real the promise that all people are created equal."

As the two of them sat in the sanctuary where Dr. King had once preached, the weight of that promise seemed to settle around them like a benediction. Outside, the city hummed with its daily struggles and small victories, each one part of the long arc of justice that still required their hands to bend it true.

President John F. Kennedy

John Fitzgerald Kennedy was the charismatic 35th President of the United States and youngest elected president who inspired a generation with his vision of American leadership, navigated the Cuban Missile Crisis, launched the ambitious goal of landing on the moon, and delivered the famous inaugural challenge to "ask not what your country can do for you—ask what you can do for your country" before being tragically assassinated in Dallas in 1963 at age 46.

The Eternal Flame

The late afternoon sun cast long shadows across Arlington National Cemetery as five figures stood quietly before the eternal flame. They had arrived separately but found themselves drawn together by the solemnity of the place and the weight of their shared burdens.

Jenna, a recently elected congresswoman from Massachusetts, clutched a wreath of white roses. Beside her, Andrew, a foreign service officer preparing for his first ambassadorial post, removed his hat as a gentle breeze stirred the autumn leaves. Emma, a federal judge whose confirmation hearings had been particularly contentious, stood with her hands clasped behind her back. Parker, a young White House aide still idealistic despite six months in Washington, shifted nervously from foot to foot. Mary, a veteran State Department analyst who had served through four administrations, watched the flame with the quiet patience of someone who had witnessed history's long arc.

"I come here whenever I'm facing something that feels bigger than me," Jenna said softly, placing the wreath near the headstone. "There's something about this place that puts things in perspective."

Andrew nodded, his eyes fixed on the flickering flame. "I'm leaving for Eastern Europe next month. My first real diplomatic assignment since the world started falling apart again. I keep wondering what he would have done."

"You mean with everything that's happening internationally?" Emma asked, her judicial training evident in her careful tone. "The tensions, the nuclear rhetoric starting up again?"

"Exactly. Everyone's pushing for immediate responses, decisive action. Show strength, they say. But I keep thinking about October 1962." Andrew paused, watching a group of tourists move respectfully past them. "Can you imagine the pressure he was under? Every advisor telling him to strike first, to show the Soviets we meant business. But he chose patience instead."

Parker looked up from her phone, where she'd been automatically checking messages before catching himself and putting it away. "That's what gets lost in the twenty-four-hour news cycle, isn't it? The value of thinking before reacting. Everyone wants instant responses now."

Mary smiled slightly at the young aide's observation. "I was just a child then, but my father worked at State during the missile crisis. He used to tell me about the meetings that went on for days, the careful consideration of every option. The pressure to act was enormous, but the president insisted on exploring every alternative."

Jenna shifted the roses slightly, making sure they caught the light. "That takes a different kind of courage, doesn't it? Especially when everyone's questioning whether you're strong enough for the job."

"The harder road," Andrew murmured. "I read once that he said true leadership isn't about proving your toughness—it's about being strong enough to choose the harder path when it leads away from catastrophe." He looked at Jenna. "You're facing your own version of that, aren't you? With the healthcare bill?"

Jenna sighed, her breath visible in the cooling air. "Every political consultant I've talked to says I'm committing career suicide. 'Too much too fast,' they tell me. 'You'll lose the moderates. Think about reelection.'" She touched the headstone gently. "But I keep thinking about Birmingham. About those children facing down the fire hoses."

Emma shifted uncomfortably. "The law is supposed to be above politics, but my confirmation hearings felt like a battlefield. Both sides wanting me to telegraph how I'd rule on cases that haven't even come before the court yet." She paused. "I kept thinking about his approach to judicial appointments—looking for people with integrity rather than predictable votes."

"You think he would have told you to wait?" Parker asked Jenna, then immediately looked embarrassed by her boldness in addressing a congresswoman so directly.

"I think he learned that some things can't wait," Jenna replied kindly. "Moral leadership can't be postponed forever in the name of political convenience. People shouldn't have to wait for their basic dignity—whether that's civil rights in the '60s or healthcare in 2025."

Mary nodded slowly. "I've watched this cycle repeat itself for decades. There's always a reason to delay, always political cover for inaction. But the problems don't wait for convenient timing."

A young father walked by with his daughter, pointing out the eternal flame and whispering something about presidents and service. They all watched the pair pass before Andrew spoke again.

"You know what strikes me most about studying his presidency? How he handled failure. The Bay of Pigs could have destroyed him, but somehow it made him better."

"How do you mean?" Emma asked.

"He didn't let it paralyze him. He learned from it—fast—and used those lessons during the missile crisis." Andrew tucked his hat under his arm. "I'm terrified of making mistakes in this new role, but maybe that's the wrong approach. Maybe the goal should be learning from them faster than your enemies can exploit them."

Parker looked relieved. "That's reassuring to hear from someone with your experience. I make mistakes daily—sometimes hourly. I keep waiting for someone to realize I don't belong here."

Mary chuckled softly. "Girl, if you're not making mistakes, you're not taking on anything important enough to matter. I've seen staffers who never fail because they never attempt anything meaningful."

Emma smiled slightly. "In law school, we studied his brother's approach to the Justice Department. He wasn't afraid to take on cases others considered too risky, too divisive. Sometimes the law requires you to stand in uncomfortable places."

Jenna looked at the younger woman with interest. "I keep second-guessing every decision, wondering if I'm being naive or idealistic."

"Or maybe you're investing in the impossible," Andrew suggested. "The moon landing must have seemed like political suicide too when he announced it. The money wasn't there, the technology didn't exist, people thought it was a waste."

"But it inspired an entire generation," Emma finished. "My grandfather still talks about watching Neil Armstrong on television. Says it made him believe America could do anything if we set our minds to it."

Parker pulled out her phone again, then caught herself and smiled sheepishly. "Sorry. Reflexive action. But that makes me think—we're so focused on the immediate news cycle, on what trends today. There's something powerful about setting goals that might take a decade to achieve."

Mary gazed thoughtfully at the flame. "Long-term thinking has become almost revolutionary. I've watched administrations change course every two years based on polling data. But the great achievements—civil rights, space exploration, rebuilding Europe after the war—those took sustained commitment."

The cemetery was growing quieter as evening approached. A groundskeeper moved respectfully in the distance, tending to other graves with quiet efficiency.

"I wonder what he'd say about staying connected to real people," Jenna mused. "It's so easy to get caught up in the Washington bubble, in the politics and the polls. But every vote I cast affects real families."

Andrew nodded thoughtfully. "In diplomacy too. It's easy to think in terms of nations and strategies, but behind every policy are individual people whose lives hang in the balance. He seemed to understand that the presidency could insulate you from the human cost of your decisions if you let it."

Emma's expression grew serious. "From the bench, you see that clearly. Every case represents someone's life, their future, their family. The law isn't abstract when you're the one making the final decision."

Parker looked uncomfortable. "That's what I struggle with most. I write memos and talking points, but I've never lived the consequences of the policies I help shape. How do you stay grounded when you're removed from the real impact?"

Mary placed a gentle hand on her shoulder. "You ask that question. You keep asking it. The moment you stop worrying about that disconnect is the moment you become part of the problem."

"The burden of service," Jenna said quietly. "I'm starting to understand what that phrase really means."

They stood in comfortable silence for a moment, watching the eternal flame dance in the growing dusk.

"Can I tell you something?" Andrew said eventually. "I almost turned down this assignment. My father kept pushing me to take something safer, more prestigious. 'Don't risk your career on a difficult post,' he said. But I realized I was more worried about disappointing him than about doing what I thought was right."

Emma looked at him with understanding. "The weight of expectations. I get that. My whole family assumed I'd stay in private practice—safe, lucrative, predictable. They didn't understand why I wanted to be a judge."

Jenna nodded. "My whole family assumed I'd follow the traditional path—safe districts, party-line votes, careful positioning for higher office."

Parker shifted nervously. "My parents still don't really understand what I do. They ask when I'm going to get a 'real job' with better security."

Mary smiled. "After forty years in government, my sister still asks when I'm going to retire and do something more relaxing. As if serving your country was supposed to be a temporary phase."

"What changed your mind?" Jenna asked Andrew.

"I realized I was spending more time trying to impress people than listening to my own judgment. More focused on appearing decisive than being thoughtful." He paused. "I think he would have understood that struggle—living up to a family name, proving yourself worthy."

Emma nodded slowly. "The confirmation process taught me something about that. You can't control how others perceive your choices, but you can control whether those choices align with your principles."

Andrew smiled ruefully. "My wife keeps reminding me that our kids are watching how I handle this. Whether I choose based on fear or conviction." He looked back at the headstone. "I think he'd say that being present with the people who matter most can't be postponed either."

Parker looked around at the group. "Is it strange that I feel less alone just standing here with all of you? Washington can be so isolating."

Mary's expression softened. "Service connects us across generations, across party lines, across different branches of government. We're all trying to do right by the country, even when we disagree on what that means."

The first stars were beginning to appear in the darkening sky. Other visitors had left, and the cemetery felt peaceful, almost sacred in its quiet.

"You know what gives me hope?" Jenna said as they prepared to leave. "He faced impossible challenges too—nuclear war, civil rights, the space race, the Cold War. But he never stopped believing in America's future, in democracy itself."

"The work is never finished," Andrew agreed. "Each generation has to take up the task again, find ways to expand liberty and justice while meeting their own particular challenges."

Emma pulled her coat tighter. "And each of us, in our own roles, carries a piece of that responsibility. Whether we're writing laws, interpreting them, implementing them, or explaining them to the public."

Parker looked back at the flame. "I think I understand now why you all come here. It's not just about him—it's about remembering what we're part of, what we're trying to continue."

Mary nodded approvingly. "Now you're beginning to understand the weight and the privilege of public service."

Jenna gathered her coat around her. "I think he'd tell us to trust our instincts, learn from our mistakes quickly, and remember that patience can be the highest form of courage."

"And that great nations must set great goals," Andrew added, "even when—especially when—we're not sure they can be achieved."

Emma looked around at the group one more time. "And that we don't have to carry these burdens alone. The work is bigger than any one person."

As they walked back toward the cemetery entrance together, five public servants from different generations and different branches of government, Jenna looked over her shoulder one more time at the eternal flame, still burning steadily against the night.

"Thank you," she whispered to the darkness.

The flame flickered on, a steady reminder that some lights refuse to be extinguished, and that the conversation between past and future never truly ends—carried forward by each new generation willing to take up the work of democracy.

Lucille Ball

Lucille Ball revolutionized television comedy and shattered barriers for women in entertainment, becoming the first female head of a major television studio while creating timeless physical comedy that continues to influence performers and delight audiences decades after her groundbreaking work on "I Love Lucy."

I Love Lucy

The flea market buzzed with weekend shoppers, but Nancy barely noticed the noise as she clutched the oversized chef's hat, still amazed at her find. Around the small café table, her research group had gathered—Eleanor with her stack of vintage Hollywood magazines, Katy adjusting her thick-rimmed glasses as she scrolled through her tablet of Lucy Ball interviews, Karaline sketching costume details in her art pad, and Elle organizing her collection of newspaper clippings. Across from them all sat Vance, stirring his coffee slowly, his hands steady as he considered Nancy's question.

"You know," Nancy said, leaning forward with excitement while her friends listened intently, "we've all been researching Lucy for years, but I never expected to meet the grandson of someone who actually worked with her. What was she really like?"

Eleanor set down her magazine and pushed her silver hair behind her ear. "I've read every biography, but nothing beats firsthand accounts."

Vance's eyes crinkled with the memory of countless stories. "According to my granddad, sharp as a tack, that one. People saw Lucy Ricardo fumbling around on screen and thought that was Lucy Ball, but let me tell you—nothing could be further from the truth. Granddad used to say she ran that set like a general, knew every camera angle, every light cue." He paused, sipping his coffee. "But she never made anyone feel small about it. She just expected excellence from everyone, including herself."

Katy looked up from her tablet. "That matches what Jess Oppenheimer said in his interviews. I heard she was incredibly driven, especially for a woman in those days."

"Driven doesn't begin to cover it." Vance chuckled. "Granddad told me about this one day when some network executive was giving her grief about a script decision. She listened politely, nodded along, then did exactly what she'd planned to do anyway. When he complained later, she just said, 'I didn't ask for permission—I just did what the show needed.' That's how Granddad ended up with this hat, actually—Lucy gave it to him after that chocolate factory episode, said he deserved something special for putting up with all her rehearsals."

Karaline stopped sketching and gestured to the hat. "The attention to detail in these costumes was incredible. Look at the stitching, the way it's constructed to hold its shape even through all that physical comedy."

Elle spread out several newspaper clippings. "I found these reviews from the chocolate factory episode. The critics were blown away by her timing." She pointed to a highlighted quote. "This one says, 'Miss Ball's pratfalls appear effortless, but closer observation reveals a master craftswoman at work.'"

Nancy pulled out her notebook, unable to help herself. "So what do you think she'd tell someone today about being successful?"

Vance was quiet for a moment, his gaze drifting over the bustling flea market where Eleanor was now examining a vintage Life magazine featuring Lucy on the cover. "Well, based on everything Granddad told me about working with her, first thing she'd say is stop waiting around for someone to tell you it's okay to chase what you want. Lucy used to tell my granddad there weren't any rules for women in television because nobody had bothered writing them yet—and she treated that like a blessing, not an obstacle."

Eleanor nodded emphatically. "That's exactly what I needed to hear. I've been wanting to start my own vintage costume business, but I keep waiting for the 'right' time."

"Don't wait," Vance continued, leaning back in his plastic chair. "She'd tell you that being persistent matters more than being naturally gifted. Granddad always said Lucy wasn't the prettiest actress in Hollywood, and she knew it. But she was willing to work harder than anyone else, willing to take the physical comedy that other actresses wouldn't touch. He watched her rehearse that chocolate factory scene until every stumble was perfect."

"That's the one where she's trying to wrap the chocolates?" Karaline gestured to the chef's hat while making quick sketches of its shape and proportions.

"That's the one. Granddad used to say people think physical comedy just happens, but Lucy would drill those bits until they were flawless. She believed the audience deserved perfection, even when she was playing someone who couldn't do anything right." Vance smiled. "Especially then. Granddad said she'd practice the same three-second gag for hours."

Katy was furiously taking notes on her tablet. "This aligns with what William Frawley said about her work ethic. He mentioned she'd rehearse until her co-stars were exhausted, but she'd still be going."

Nancy scribbled notes alongside Katy. "What about the business side? Running Desilu couldn't have been easy."

Vance's expression grew more serious while Elle organized her clippings about Lucy's business ventures. "Granddad watched her transform from performer to executive, and he said she'd tell any woman in business today that you have to be twice as prepared and three times as determined to get half the respect men take for granted. When Lucy was the only woman in those boardroom meetings, she couldn't afford to be wrong about the details. Granddad said she knew every number, every contract, every technical specification."

Eleanor leaned forward, her eyes bright with interest. "That's incredibly inspiring. I worry about the business side of things."

"You'd be perfect at it," Elle encouraged her friend, then turned back to Vance. "I've read that Desilu produced Star Trek. Lucy essentially green-lit one of the most influential science fiction series ever made."

Vance nodded. "Granddad was there for some of those meetings. But here's something interesting—Granddad told me she once said she spent too many years trying to prove she could think like a man. Said her biggest breakthrough came when she realized that thinking like a woman—with intuition, with emotional intelligence—was actually her greatest strength. Women bring something different to the table, she'd say, and that difference has value."

Karaline looked up from her sketching. "That's surprisingly progressive for the 1950s."

"Lucy was ahead of her time in a lot of ways." Vance's voice softened. "But Granddad said she'd also tell you not to sacrifice everything for success. He saw how she and Desi had magic together, professionally and personally, but mixing love and business put strains on their relationship. Granddad once overheard her say that if she could change anything, she'd find a better balance between ambition and heart."

Katy adjusted her glasses, looking thoughtful. "What do you mean?"

Vance stirred his coffee thoughtfully while the five women waited attentively. "Granddad always said Lucy was incredibly strong, incredibly independent. Had to be, in that business. But he thought sometimes she held people at arm's length when she should have let them closer. He believed she'd tell young people today that strength and vulnerability aren't opposites—even though it took her most of a lifetime to figure that out."

Nancy felt a pang of recognition, and noticed Eleanor nodding knowingly. "That sounds familiar."

"She'd also tell you to maintain your own identity, especially in partnerships. Granddad could see how much Lucy loved Desi, but he thought she sometimes lost herself trying to be what she thought he needed instead of staying true to who she was." Vance shook his head. "Granddad used to say success is wonderful, but it's not much fun if you don't have someone special to share it with."

Elle gathered her clippings into a neat pile. "That's why what you five have is so special," Vance observed, gesturing to the women around the table. "You're sharing this passion together."

The afternoon sun filtered through the café's plastic awning as Vance continued. "About the work itself—Granddad said Lucy believed comedy should come from love, not anger. You can be silly without being cruel, funny without tearing people down. She thought that was important work, making people laugh. Said people need it."

Karaline nodded enthusiastically. "In my art classes, I try to capture that same joy. Comedy as healing."

"And collaboration?" Katy asked, looking up from her tablet where she'd been cross-referencing quotes.

"Everything to Lucy, according to Granddad. She surrounded herself with people who were smarter than her in their areas of expertise, listened to their ideas, never let ego get in the way of making the best possible product. Granddad said some of her biggest successes came from ideas that weren't originally hers, but she was smart enough to recognize them and support them."

Eleanor smiled. "Like how we all bring different strengths to our research group."

Nancy closed her notebook, feeling like they'd all just received a masterclass filtered through generations. "Anything else?"

Vance smiled, that twinkle returning to his eyes as he looked around at the five eager faces. "Granddad always said she'd tell you never to underestimate the intelligence of your audience, but never overestimate their patience either. And no matter what happens, no matter how hard it gets—" He gestured around the cheerful chaos of the flea market, where vendors were laughing with customers and children were running between the stalls. "—remember to laugh along the way. Granddad said she believed life's too short not to."

As they sat there, watching the world go by, Nancy realized she was holding more than just a prop from a famous TV show. She was carrying forward the wisdom of a woman who had blazed trails and made mistakes, filtered through the observations of a prop man who had watched it all unfold, and now passed down to his grandson and shared with five women who would carry these lessons forward together.

Elle carefully packed away her clippings. "We should document all of this properly."

"I'm already planning a whole series of paintings inspired by this conversation," Karaline said, showing them her sketches of the chef's hat from different angles.

Katy looked up from her tablet. "I'll compile all the quotes we've gathered today with the ones I already have. This could become a real resource for others."

Eleanor held one of her vintage magazines thoughtfully. "And I'm definitely starting that costume business. Lucy would have told me to stop making excuses."

Vance glanced at his watch and pushed back from the table. "Well, I should probably get back to my table before someone makes off with my merchandise."

"Of course," Nancy said, standing as well along with her friends. "Your grandfather must have been a wonderful man to have observed Lucy so closely, to have remembered all those details about what she said and believed."

Vance paused, his hand resting on the back of his chair. For a moment, he seemed to be wrestling with something internal. Then he looked directly at the five women, his expression suddenly vulnerable.

"You know, I've never told anyone this before, but I think the real reason Granddad knew so much about Lucy, why he paid such close attention to everything she said and did..." He took a deep breath. "I think he had a bit of a crush on her. Nothing inappropriate, mind you. He loved my grandmother dearly, and he never would have acted on it. But I could see it sometimes, in the way his eyes would light up when he talked about her, the way he'd save every little story, every observation."

The five women exchanged glances, each feeling the weight of this intimate family secret.

Nancy felt a wave of tenderness for this man sharing such a personal revelation. "That makes it even more special, doesn't it? All those memories, all that wisdom—it was preserved by someone who truly admired her."

Elle nodded softly. "Love—even unspoken love—has a way of seeing clearly."

Vance nodded, a soft smile crossing his face. "I think so too. Granddad knew it couldn't go anywhere, and he was too much of a gentleman to even try. But maybe that's why he saw her so clearly—he could appreciate her strength, her vulnerability, her contradictions, without any agenda except genuine respect." He picked up the chef's hat gently. "Makes this old thing feel even more precious, knowing it came from someone who really understood what she was trying to accomplish."

As Vance walked back toward his table, the five friends stood there for a moment, each holding their piece of the afternoon—Nancy with her notebook, Eleanor with her magazines, Katy with her tablet, Karaline with her sketches, and Elle with her carefully organized clippings.

"We should meet next week to go through everything we learned today," Eleanor suggested.

"My place," Katy offered. "I'll have all the digital files organized by then."

"And I'll bring coffee and pastries," Elle added with a grin. "Lucy would have approved of treating research like a celebration."

Karaline was already sketching again, capturing the five of them around the table. "This whole afternoon felt like Lucy brought us together through time—her wisdom, filtered through a man who loved her quietly, preserved by his grandson, and now shared among friends who'll carry it forward."

Nancy looked around at her research partners, realizing that they'd found something more valuable than any collectible. They'd discovered that the most beautiful stories unfold in community, in the spaces between what we expect and what we discover when we're open to learning from each other.

Sometimes, she thought, the most profound discoveries happen when we're surrounded by people who share our passions and help us see familiar stories through new eyes. The chef's hat suddenly felt less like a collectible and more like a responsibility—a tangible link to lessons worth preserving and sharing, together.

Walter Cronkite

Walter Cronkite, known as "the most trusted man in America," served as CBS Evening News anchor for nearly two decades and became the definitive voice of American journalism, guiding the nation through pivotal moments from the Kennedy assassination to the moon landing with unparalleled credibility and integrity.

And that's the Way it Is

The newsroom hummed with its usual pre-broadcast energy. Monitors flickered with feeds from around the world, and the faint scent of coffee mingled with the sterile air of the television studio. Sue shuffled through her notes one final time, then glanced at the clock—forty minutes until they went live.

"All set for the weekend?" she asked her co-anchor, Larry, who was adjusting his tie and reviewing his teleprompter script.

Larry sighed and leaned back in his chair. "Well, my original plans just got derailed. I was looking forward to eighteen holes at the country club and maybe just lounging by the pool, but my sister's family is flying in from Denver. So instead, I'll be playing tour guide and host."

"That doesn't sound so bad," Sue said, raising an eyebrow. "Don't you enjoy spending time with them?"

"Oh, absolutely. I love them to pieces—my niece and nephew are hilarious, and I don't get to see them nearly enough. But you know how it is when family visits. You feel like you have to entertain them every minute."

Sue started to respond, but Larry shrugged and added with a resigned smile, "That's the way it is."

Sue burst into laughter, covering her mouth as her shoulders shook.

"What's so funny?" Larry asked, genuinely puzzled.

"You just quoted one of the most famous newsmen in television history," she said, still grinning. "That was Walter Cronkite's signature sign-off. 'And that's the way it is.'"

Larry's face went blank. "Walter who?"

Sue's jaw dropped. "You're kidding me. Walter Cronkite? 'The most trusted man in America'? CBS Evening News for like, what, twenty years?"

"Before my time, I guess," Larry said sheepishly. "I mean, I think I've heard the name..."

"Larry, he was THE anchorman. He covered everything—World War II, Kennedy's assassination, the moon landing, Watergate, Vietnam. People literally planned their dinner around watching him deliver the news."

Larry leaned forward, suddenly interested. "Okay, now I'm curious. What made him so special? I mean, we all read the news, right?"

Sue glanced around the newsroom—at the multiple screens showing different cable news channels, each with their own obvious political slant, at the social media feeds scrolling endlessly with hot takes and breaking news alerts. "Cronkite had this fundamental belief that seems revolutionary now—that the truth isn't partisan. That facts aren't Democrat or Republican, they just are."

"That does sound revolutionary," Larry admitted, gesturing toward the wall of partisan coverage. "Every network has their angle now."

"Exactly. But Cronkite believed journalists should inform the public, not tell them what to think. He'd present the facts as clearly as he could and trust Americans to draw their own conclusions. Can you imagine showing that kind of restraint today?"

Larry was quiet for a moment, absently clicking his pen. "You know, sometimes I wonder what someone like that would think about what we do now. All the pressure to get ratings, to break stories first, to have the hottest take."

"I think Cronkite would say we've lost sight of journalism's civic mission," Sue replied thoughtfully. "He came from an era when news divisions were expected to serve the public interest, even when it was expensive or unpopular. He'd probably be horrified by how we prioritize clicks over substance."

"But that's the business now," Larry protested. "If we don't move fast, someone else will."

Sue shook her head. "Cronkite would say that's exactly the wrong approach. He spent decades building trust by being accurate and fair. He understood that credibility is earned slowly and lost quickly. One rushed, wrong story can destroy years of careful work."

"So what would he tell us to do differently?"

"He'd say we need to remember that our job is to serve the public, not make ourselves famous. He'd tell us to be curious about everything, to ask the questions others are afraid to ask, to listen more than we speak." Sue's voice grew more passionate. "And he'd remind us that we should never let anyone convince us that truth is negotiable or that facts are matters of opinion."

Larry looked around the newsroom with new eyes. "When you put it like that, it sounds like we've really lost our way."

"Maybe. But Cronkite also believed in the power of journalism to serve democracy. Look at how he handled Vietnam—for years he reported what officials told him, but when the evidence of his own eyes showed otherwise, he had the courage to call it a stalemate. He knew sometimes the most patriotic thing a journalist can do is tell uncomfortable truths."

"That took guts."

"It did. And Cronkite would tell us that's still our responsibility. Question authority, especially when it makes us uncomfortable. Follow the facts wherever they lead, even if powerful people don't like it."

Larry nodded slowly. "What about staying objective when everything is so emotionally charged? I mean, he covered Kennedy's assassination, the moon landing—huge emotional moments."

"That's one of the most brilliant things about Cronkite's approach," Sue said. "He understood that journalists are human beings with feelings. The key isn't to eliminate emotion but to channel it properly. When he choked up announcing Kennedy's death, when his voice betrayed excitement watching the moon landing—those genuine human responses actually made viewers trust him more, not less."

"Because it showed he took these momentous events seriously?"

"Exactly. Cronkite proved you can have authentic human reactions while still serving the story with integrity."

Larry was quiet for several minutes, then said, "You know what I keep thinking about? Here I am complaining about entertaining family this weekend, but didn't guys like Cronkite sacrifice a lot of family time for their careers?"

Sue's expression grew more serious. "Actually, that's one of the most powerful pieces of advice Cronkite ever gave. Later in life, he said if he could change one thing, it would be spending more evenings at home with his wife and children when they were young. He realized the news would have gone on without him, but those precious family moments—he could never get those back."

"Wow." Larry stared at his hands. "So even the great Walter Cronkite learned that lesson the hard way."

"He did. And he was honest enough to share that wisdom. He'd tell us that the most important stories are often the ones we live, not the ones we report."

The floor director appeared at the edge of their set. "Fifteen minutes, people."

As they began their final preparations, Larry said, "You know what? Cronkite would probably tell me to stop seeing my family visit as an obligation and start seeing it as an opportunity. To really be present instead of just going through the motions."

"I think he would," Sue agreed. "And he'd probably tell us both to approach our jobs differently too. Focus on serving democracy instead of serving our egos."

"What do you mean?"

Sue adjusted her earpiece thoughtfully. "Cronkite would say we should celebrate human achievement as readily as we expose human failure. Look for the stories that bring out the best in people, not just the scandals and conflicts that drive ratings."

"Like how he covered the space program?"

"Exactly. His enthusiasm for space exploration was genuine because it represented everything he loved about human potential. He'd tell us to find those stories today—the innovations, the acts of courage, the people making their communities better."

"That's actually refreshing," Larry said. "I'm so tired of the constant negativity."

"Cronkite understood something we've forgotten," Sue continued. "History is made by ordinary people in extraordinary circumstances. He saw it on D-Day, during the civil rights movement, at Watergate. He'd remind us to look for the human element in every story—the courage, the resilience, the dignity of people facing challenges."

Larry grinned. "You're making me want to be a better journalist."

"Cronkite would say that's the point. He'd tell us that in our age of social media and instant communication, the temptation to sacrifice long-term credibility for short-term attention is enormous. But it's a devil's bargain that benefits no one."

"So stick to the fundamentals?"

"Exactly. Accuracy over speed. Fairness over sensationalism. Service over self-promotion." Sue smiled. "He'd also remind us that the digital age has democratized information in ways that can strengthen democracy—but only if we help people distinguish between information and knowledge, between data and wisdom."

"That's our responsibility too?"

"Cronkite would say yes. In a world where anyone can claim to be a reporter, the need for genuine professional journalism becomes more important, not less."

As they settled into their chairs and waited for the red light, Larry felt something shift in his perspective. "You know what Cronkite would probably tell us right now?"

"What's that?"

"That we have forty years of television history and wisdom to draw from. That we don't have to reinvent journalism—we just have to remember why it matters."

Sue nodded. "He'd say our fundamental responsibilities remain constant: seek truth, question power, serve the common good, and remember that behind every story are human beings whose lives matter."

"The technology changes, but the principles don't?"

"That's pure Cronkite wisdom. He'd tell us that all these new tools—live broadcasts from anywhere, real-time fact-checking, multiple platforms—they're only as good as the principles that guide their use."

The red light began to flash, signaling thirty seconds to air.

"I feel like I just got a masterclass in journalism," Larry whispered.

"From one of the best," Sue whispered back. "Cronkite would tell us to go out there and prove we're worthy of the trust people place in us."

"Any final Cronkite wisdom?"

Sue smiled as the director counted down from ten. "He'd say remember that credibility is the greatest honor of our professional lives. And never forget that behind all the technology and platforms and ratings, we're just human beings trying to help other human beings understand their world."

As the cameras went live, both anchors felt a renewed sense of purpose. They weren't just reading news—they were carrying forward a tradition of public service journalism, guided by the wisdom of a man who had shown them what it meant to earn and deserve the public's trust.

The red light blazed, and they began to deliver the evening news with a newfound commitment to the Cronkite principles: accuracy, fairness, curiosity, and service. In a media landscape that often seemed to have lost its way, they had found their compass—the enduring wisdom of journalism's greatest practitioner, pointing them toward truth.

Sir Arthur Conan Doyle

Sir Arthur Conan Doyle was a British physician and author who created the legendary detective Sherlock Holmes, becoming one of the world's most influential crime writers while also pursuing real criminal investigations, historical novels, and later in life, spiritualist research.

The Game's Afoot

The monthly ZOOM meeting of the Sherlock Holmes Society is underway. Tom C adjusted his camera and looked at the gallery view showing all fifteen participants. "That's a fantastic question, Kristin. What *can* we learn from Doyle beyond his storytelling abilities?"

Sandy K was first to unmute. "Well, I think one of the biggest things is his emphasis on observation. Doyle was trained as a doctor, and he brought that same methodical precision to everything else he did. He didn't just see what was obvious—he noticed the telling details that others missed."

"That's so true," Steve M chimed in. "And it wasn't just about being observant for its own sake. He used those skills in real life to help people. Remember the George Edalji case? Doyle basically played Sherlock Holmes in real life to get an innocent man out of prison."

Daniel J nodded enthusiastically. "Yes! That case really shows how he believed in applying logic and careful investigation to actual injustice, not just fictional crimes. He put his reputation on the line to fight for someone who couldn't fight for himself."

Paul S leaned forward toward his camera. "I think there's a lesson there about standing up for what's right, even when it's inconvenient or unpopular. Doyle took on causes that cost him time, money, and sometimes friendships."

"Speaking of learning from difficulty," Ann K interjected, "I read that his early experiences as a ship's doctor on an Arctic whaler were brutal, but he later said those hardships taught him that courage isn't the absence of fear—it's taking action despite being afraid."

Doug V unmuted himself. "That reminds me of something else about Doyle—he seemed to understand that sometimes our greatest contributions aren't what we planned. He wanted to be known for his historical novels, not detective stories, but Holmes became his legacy. There's wisdom in being open to where your authentic work leads you."

Tram C spoke up. "I think he also understood the balance between knowledge and imagination. For his historical novels, he spent years researching medieval manuscripts and walking battlefields, but he knew all that research would be worthless without creativity to bring it to life."

"That's interesting," Darren S said, adjusting his headset. "But I think we should also acknowledge that Doyle wasn't perfect. He got carried away with spiritualism after losing his son in the war, and made some questionable calls—like with those fairy photographs. But even that teaches us something about being willing to admit our mistakes."

Ruth S nodded. "Exactly. He seemed to believe it was better to be wrong while seeking truth than to be right while staying silent. That takes courage."

Maurie G, who had been quietly listening, finally spoke. "You know what strikes me most about Doyle? He understood that physical and mental health go together. He played cricket, promoted skiing, stayed active. He didn't separate the body from the mind."

Jennie P smiled at her camera. "And let's not forget his advice about writing—or really, about any creative work. He said to write what interests you, not what you think will sell. Holmes was supposed to be a minor character, but because Doyle wrote authentically, that character took on a life of its own."

Pete J, who had been taking notes throughout, finally unmuted. "I think if I had to sum up what we can learn from Doyle, it's this combination of careful observation with passionate purpose. Be methodical in your thinking but don't lose your sense of wonder. Question authority, but do it from knowledge, not just skepticism."

Steve S, who had been quiet for most of the discussion, added, "There's one more thing I'd mention. From what I've read about his later reflections, he regretted not spending more time with his children when they were young. Success in public life couldn't make up for missing those private family moments. That might be his most important lesson—remembering that your most important stories are the ones you live with the people you love."

The Zoom room fell silent for a moment as that sentiment settled in.

Tom C looked at the gallery view again and smiled. "Wow, Kristin, your question really opened up something rich here. It sounds like Doyle has as much to teach us about living as he does about writing mysteries."

Kristin, who had started it all, grinned. "This is exactly what I was hoping for. It makes me want to read more about his actual life, not just his stories."

"Well," Tom said, glancing at his notes, "I think that's a perfect segue into our next agenda item..."

Marilyn Monroe

Marilyn Monroe transformed herself from Norma Jeane Baker into one of the most enduring cultural icons of the 20th century, yet her greatest tragedy was that beneath the carefully crafted image of glamour and sexuality lived a deeply intelligent and sensitive woman whose authentic self was often overshadowed by the very fame she had sought as an escape from childhood pain.

Beyond the Image

The Turner Classic Movies studio felt unusually quiet for a Thursday evening. Host Chris adjusted his tie nervously as he reviewed his notes one final time. Tonight's feature, "Some Like It Hot," promised to draw their largest audience of the month, but Chris felt underprepared. His usual confident demeanor wavered as he glanced at the clock—thirty minutes until showtime.

Elizabeth from UCLA's Film Studies department entered the green room carrying a worn leather satchel and an air of scholarly authority. She'd been studying Monroe's career for over two decades, and Chris had specifically requested her expertise for tonight's discussion.

Behind her came Carla, the show's senior producer, carrying a tablet and wearing her signature oversized glasses. She'd worked in television for thirty years and had actually met Monroe briefly at a Hollywood party in the early sixties. Dan, the show's head cameraman and occasional on-air contributor, followed them in, already checking lighting angles.

"Elizabeth, thank you for coming on such short notice," Chris said, rising to shake her hand. "I have to admit, I'm feeling a bit out of my depth here. I mean, other than being a beautiful woman, what else could Marilyn really have to offer modern viewers? And what kind of life advice could someone like that possibly give about being successful?"

Carla winced audibly from where she was setting up her tablet. "Chris, honey, if you go on air with that attitude, our ratings won't be the only thing crashing tonight."

Elizabeth set down her satchel and studied Chris's face carefully. She recognized the tone—the same dismissive attitude she'd encountered countless times in academic circles when Monroe's name came up.

"Chris, may I call you Chris?" she began, settling into the chair across from him. "That question tells me exactly why tonight's discussion is so important. You're starting with the most common misconception about Marilyn Monroe."

Chris leaned forward, genuinely curious now. "Which is?"

"That she was just a beautiful woman who got lucky. The truth is far more complex and, frankly, far more valuable to your viewers." Elizabeth pulled out a notebook filled with years of research. "Monroe was acutely aware of how the world saw her—as a product, a fantasy, a commodity. But she spent her entire career fighting against those limitations."

Dan set down his light meter and interjected, "I've been filming classic Hollywood retrospectives for fifteen years, and Monroe's footage always stands out. The way she commands the camera—that's not luck. That's craft."

"Exactly," Elizabeth agreed. "Take tonight's film, for instance. By the time she made 'Some Like It Hot,' Monroe had already started her own production company. She was one of the first major stars to challenge the studio system directly. She understood that if she didn't take control of her own career, others would continue to define her worth solely by her appearance."

Chris made a note. "That's actually quite progressive for the late fifties."

Carla looked up from her tablet. "My mother worked as a script supervisor at Fox during that era. The stories she told about Monroe—the woman fought battles with studio heads that would have destroyed lesser talents. She insisted on creative control when no one gave actresses that kind of power."

"Exactly. And her advice to modern viewers? Well, she learned some hard lessons about the importance of knowing yourself versus trying to become what everyone else wants you to be." Elizabeth's voice grew more animated. "She once talked about spending years trying to please everyone—directors, studio executives, the public. She discovered that this path leads to a kind of emptiness, even when you achieve everything you thought you wanted."

"That's surprisingly profound," Chris admitted.

"Monroe would tell your viewers to learn to say no, and learn it early. She spent too much of her career accepting roles and situations that didn't serve her because she was afraid of disappointing people. The cost was enormous—not just professionally, but personally."

Elizabeth flipped through her notes. "She also understood something crucial about success that many people miss: fame can become a prison if you're not careful about who holds the keys. She talked about losing herself in the image she'd created, about forgetting where 'Marilyn Monroe' ended and Norma Jeane began."

"So what would she suggest as an alternative?"

"Authenticity, above all else. She'd tell people to trust their instincts, to value their own opinions above others', and to find work that feeds the soul, not just the bank account. Monroe spent her later years studying at the Actors Studio, doing the most honest and vulnerable work of her career. She discovered that using your own struggles and pain to create something truthful—whether in art or in life—was far more fulfilling than maintaining a perfect image."

Chris was scribbling notes furiously now. "This is fascinating. What about the personal side? The relationships?"

Dan paused his equipment check. "If I can add something—I once filmed an interview with one of her Actors Studio classmates. She said Monroe was always asking questions, always trying to understand the emotional truth of a scene. She wasn't the dumb blonde everyone assumed."

"Thank you, Dan. That's exactly right," Elizabeth continued. "She learned that love shouldn't require you to diminish yourself to make someone else comfortable. Her marriages taught her that even well-meaning people sometimes want to protect you in ways that feel like another kind of cage. She'd probably tell your viewers to be wary of anyone who claims to love you while asking you to be less than who you are."

Elizabeth checked her watch—fifteen minutes to air. "Perhaps most importantly, Monroe understood that the love and acceptance we seek from the world can never fill the emptiness left by the love we don't give ourselves. She'd tell people to be kinder to themselves, to guard their inner lives fiercely, and to create spaces that exist entirely separate from their public personas."

"That's remarkably wise advice," Chris said, his initial skepticism completely replaced by genuine respect. "Anything else?"

"Education. Monroe was largely self-taught, but she read voraciously—philosophy, poetry, psychology. She understood that knowledge is the one thing no one can take from you, and it's the best defense against those who would try to manipulate or diminish you."

Carla closed her tablet and joined the conversation circle. "When I met her at that party in '61, she was carrying a book of Rilke poems. I was just a production assistant then, barely twenty years old. She actually talked to me—really talked, asked about my ambitions, gave me advice about navigating the industry as a woman. She told me to document everything, keep records, never let anyone make me feel small. I've never forgotten it."

Chris closed his notebook and looked at Elizabeth with new appreciation. "I have to confess, I came into this thinking we'd spend most of our time talking about her look, her marriages, maybe the mystery surrounding her death. Instead, you've shown me someone who was remarkably insightful about the human condition."

"That's exactly the point, Chris. Monroe's greatest tragedy wasn't her death—it was that so few people saw her clearly while she was alive. But her greatest gift to us is the wisdom that came from her struggles. She learned to see through the illusions of fame and success to understand what really matters: authentic self-love, meaningful work, genuine relationships, and the courage to live your own truth rather than someone else's expectations."

As they settled into the studio chairs for a final sound check, Chris glanced at his additional notes. "Elizabeth, there's one aspect of Monroe's life that I know our viewers will be curious about—her relationships with powerful men, particularly President Kennedy. What do you think drove those connections?"

Dan was adjusting the main camera angle when he spoke up. "If we're going there, we should be careful. I've seen too many documentaries reduce her to gossip fodder. Let's make sure we're treating her with respect."

"Absolutely," Elizabeth agreed, pausing thoughtfully and choosing her words carefully. "That's where Monroe's story becomes even more complex, Chris. She discovered that fame could open doors to circles of power she never could have imagined as Norma Jeane Baker. But she also learned a harsh lesson about the nature of those relationships."

"Which was?"

"That many powerful people were drawn not to her, but to what she represented—the fantasy, the symbol. They wanted to possess a piece of that image, to own something that the entire world desired. It was intoxicating, certainly, but also deeply isolating."

Chris leaned in. "So you think her motives were about access to power?"

"Partly, yes. Monroe was far more politically aware than people gave her credit for. She was genuinely interested in world affairs, in the intellectual conversations that happened in those circles. But I think there was something deeper at play." Elizabeth adjusted her glasses. "Remember, this was a woman who had spent her childhood feeling abandoned, unloved. The attention of the most powerful man in the world must have felt like ultimate validation."

"A kind of healing for old wounds?"

"Exactly. But Monroe was intelligent enough to recognize the trap. She realized that even at the highest levels of power and influence, people rarely wanted to know the real person underneath the image. They wanted Marilyn Monroe the fantasy, not the complicated, thoughtful, struggling woman she actually was."

Carla interjected softly, "She told me something that night we met. She said, 'Everyone wants to know Marilyn, but nobody wants to know Norma Jeane.' I didn't fully understand it then, but now..." She trailed off, shaking her head.

Elizabeth pulled out another set of notes. "She talked about learning to be careful about who she trusted with her private thoughts and feelings. These relationships taught her that fame can make you a target—not just for exploitation, but for people who want to collect you like a trophy."

"That must have been incredibly lonely," Chris observed.

"Devastatingly so. Imagine being desired by some of the most powerful people in the world, yet feeling completely unseen by them. Monroe came to understand that these men were often more interested in the thrill of the conquest, the bragging rights, than in her as a human being. The President, for instance—she recognized that she was essentially a beautiful distraction from the enormous pressures of his office."

Chris made more notes. "So what did she learn from those experiences?"

"That proximity to power doesn't equal personal empowerment. If anything, it can make you more vulnerable. Monroe found herself navigating dangerous political waters, becoming inadvertently entangled in situations that were far beyond her control. She learned that when you're involved with people at that level, you become part of their story whether you want to or not."

"And the personal cost?"

"Enormous. She realized she was seeking something from these relationships that they could never provide—genuine love and acceptance. The excitement of being desired by powerful men was intoxicating, but it was also empty. It reinforced the very thing she was trying to escape: being valued primarily for her image rather than her substance."

Elizabeth glanced at the cameras being adjusted around them. "Monroe would probably tell your viewers to be very wary of relationships where the other person seems more interested in what you represent than who you are. She learned that even presidents and powerful men can be emotionally unavailable, can use their status to avoid real intimacy."

"That's a sobering lesson."

Dan finished his camera adjustments and added, "We see it all the time in this industry—people who chase proximity to fame or power thinking it will somehow complete them. It never does. Monroe figured that out, even if it took her whole life to learn it."

"Yes, but also a valuable one," Elizabeth continued. "Monroe discovered that true connection requires vulnerability from both parties. In relationships with such extreme power imbalances, genuine vulnerability becomes almost impossible. The powerful person has too much to lose, and the other person—even someone as famous as Monroe—becomes the one taking all the emotional risks."

Chris nodded thoughtfully. "It sounds like she came to see these relationships as another form of performance."

"That's very perceptive, Chris. Yes, she did. She realized she was playing a role even in her most intimate moments—being the exciting, glamorous woman who could provide escape and fantasy. But that meant her real self, with all her fears and insecurities and deep thoughts, remained hidden and unacknowledged."

Elizabeth closed her notebook. "Perhaps most importantly, Monroe learned that seeking validation from external sources—even the most prestigious ones—can never fill the internal void. The President's attention, the thrill of moving in those circles of power, the sense of being special and chosen—none of it addressed her fundamental need to love and value herself."

"So her advice to viewers would be?"

"Don't mistake being desired for being loved. Don't confuse access to power with personal empowerment. And most crucially, don't sacrifice your authentic self for the excitement of being part of someone else's story, no matter how glamorous or important that story might seem."

Carla checked her watch and signaled to Chris. "Two minutes to air, everyone."

Chris looked up from his notes. "Elizabeth, this conversation has completely changed how I understand Monroe's life. She wasn't just a victim of powerful men—she was someone trying to navigate impossible situations while learning hard truths about human nature."

"Exactly. And her relationships with figures like Kennedy, viewed in this light, become less about scandal and more about a brilliant woman's education in the realities of power, fame, and the human heart. Her real wisdom came from recognizing that even the most extraordinary external validation couldn't substitute for the work of understanding and accepting herself."

Dan gave a thumbs up from behind the main camera. "We're ready when you are."

Carla smiled at the group. "This is going to be one of our best shows. I can feel it. Monroe would be proud to be discussed this way—as the complex, intelligent woman she actually was."

As the studio lights came up and the opening music began, Chris felt prepared to present Monroe not as a tabloid figure, but as a woman whose experiences with the most powerful people of her era had taught her profound lessons about authenticity, self-worth, and the courage to seek genuine connection rather than mere admiration.

"Places, everyone," called the director. Tonight's discussion would reveal Marilyn Monroe as she truly was: not just a beautiful woman who happened to know famous people, but a complex individual whose relationships with power taught her invaluable lessons about what really matters in life.

From his position behind the camera, Dan adjusted the final shot, while Carla watched from the control room, both knowing they were about to be part of something special—a conversation that honored Monroe's true legacy.

Prime Minister Margaret Thatcher

Margaret Thatcher was Britain's first female Prime Minister who earned the nickname "The Iron Lady" for her uncompromising leadership as she transformed Britain through free-market reforms, privatization, and victory in the Falklands War, becoming a global icon of conservative politics.

The Iron Test

The late afternoon sun slanted through the tall windows of the private committee room, casting long shadows across the polished mahogany table. JoAnne sat straight-backed in her chair, her hands clasped in her lap, facing three senior party officials. The weight of the moment pressed down on her—being invited to consider a run for Parliament was beyond anything she'd dared imagine when she'd first donned her barrister's wig five years ago.

"JoAnne," began Keaton, the party chairman, his fingers steepled before him. "We've been watching your career with considerable interest. Your work on the Henderson case, your speeches at the Young Conservatives—you have something we haven't seen in a long time."

"What exactly do you mean, Keaton?" JoAnne asked, though she suspected she knew where this was heading.

"Fire," said Ava, the chief whip, leaning forward. "Conviction. The willingness to take unpopular positions when you know they're right. We see echoes of Margaret Thatcher in you."

JoAnne felt her cheeks warm. "That's... quite a comparison. I'm not sure I understand what that means, exactly."

Keaton exchanged a glance with his colleagues. "Perhaps we should explain what we mean by that. What made the Iron Lady so formidable wasn't just her policies—it was her approach to leadership itself."

"The first thing you must understand," Ava continued, "is that leadership isn't a popularity contest. Margaret once said that you should never mistake consensus for truth, nor popularity for righteousness. When she privatized industries that had been in state hands for generations, when she stood against the miners' strikes, half the country thought she was going too far. But she understood that making difficult decisions—decisions others lack the courage to make—that's what leadership truly means."

JoAnne nodded slowly. "I suppose that's what drew me to law in the first place. Sometimes you have to argue unpopular positions because they're correct."

"Precisely," said Harrison, the third official, who had been silent until now. "But it goes deeper than that. Take the Falklands. Many advised negotiation, compromise, some face-saving diplomatic solution. But eight hundred British citizens had been invaded, and no amount of diplomatic nicety could paper over that fundamental violation. Principles mean nothing if you lack the will to defend them."

"She understood something else crucial," Ava added. "Economic freedom and political freedom are inseparable. You cannot have one without the other for very long. When we talk about returning power to the people, we don't just mean voting—we mean giving ordinary citizens a stake in the success of their country's enterprise."

Keaton leaned back in his chair. "But here's what you must be prepared for, JoAnne. Leadership often requires you to stand alone. During the European budget negotiations, she refused to accept the outrageous contributions Britain was being asked to make. 'I want my money back,' she told them. Many in her own party thought she was being unnecessarily confrontational, but she wouldn't budge until Britain got a fair settlement."

JoAnne felt a flutter of anxiety. "Standing alone sounds rather... lonely."

"It is," Ava said quietly. "The loneliness of command isn't merely a phrase—it's a daily reality. When that bomb went off in Brighton, trying to kill her and the entire Cabinet, she could have retreated. Instead, she proceeded with the conference the next morning. Because to do otherwise would have been surrender."

"But," Harrison interjected, "she also taught us that even good ideas can fail if they're poorly executed or inadequately explained. The poll tax was sound in principle—why should a duke and a dustman pay the same rates simply because they lived in the same area? But the implementation was a disaster. Leadership requires not just conviction, but wisdom in practice."

Keaton studied JoAnne's face. "What we're asking you to consider isn't easy. It demands intellectual honesty above all else. You must be willing to change your mind when evidence demands it, but not simply because the wind has shifted. Conviction politics means trusting your instincts and standing by your principles."

"There's something else," Ava added, her voice softer now. "The personal cost. A political career demands sacrifices that extend far beyond the political arena. Margaret herself would tell you—if she were here—that the demands of public life, the constant scrutiny, the security concerns, they shape not just your life but your family's life in ways that aren't always fair."

JoAnne was quiet for a long moment, absorbing their words. "So when you say I remind you of her..."

"We mean you have the potential for that kind of principled leadership," Keaton said. "The question is: do you have the stomach for it? Can you make the difficult decisions? Can you stand alone when necessary? Can you trust your instincts even when the polls say otherwise?"

JoAnne looked around the room, at these three people who held so much influence over the direction of the party, of the country. Outside, London hummed with the business of ordinary life—people heading home from work, families gathering for dinner, children playing in parks. All of them depending, whether they knew it or not, on the decisions made in rooms like this one.

"I think," she said finally, "that if you're not prepared to do those things—to stand alone, to make unpopular decisions, to put principles before popularity—then you have no business seeking to lead."

The three officials exchanged knowing looks.

"JoAnne," Keaton said, a smile playing at the corners of his mouth, "I think we may have found our candidate."

As the meeting concluded and JoAnne gathered her things, she couldn't shake the feeling that she was standing at a crossroads. The path they were offering led toward power, yes, but also toward a kind of isolation she'd never experienced. The Iron Lady's legacy wasn't just one of political achievement—it was a testament to the price of unwavering conviction.

Walking through the corridors of Parliament toward the exit, JoAnne wondered if she truly had the strength to pay that price. Time, she supposed, would tell.

Jackie Robinson

Jackie Robinson broke baseball's color barrier when he became the first Black player in Major League Baseball's modern era with the Brooklyn Dodgers in 1947, enduring tremendous racism with dignity and courage while helping to pave the way for the broader civil rights movement through his athletic excellence and unwavering commitment to equality.

Hot Dogs and Heroes

The steam rose from Ben's hot dog cart like incense in the crisp October air outside the Plaza Hotel in New York City. He'd been working this corner for nearly thirty years, watching the parade of tourists and locals flow past his little aluminum kingdom. Today, three customers had gathered at his cart—a man in an expensive-looking jacket, clearly out of place with his West Coast casualness, and two young women who appeared to be sisters, both wearing Columbia University hoodies.

"I'll take one with everything," the visitor said, his slight accent marking him as California born and raised.

"Two with mustard and relish," added the taller of the two young women, her dark hair pulled back in a ponytail. "I'm Juniper, by the way, and this is my sister Ivy."

"You got it," Ben replied, expertly maneuvering his tongs. As he worked, a group of kids walked by wearing Dodgers caps, probably tourists from some school trip. The sight made him smile, and he nodded toward them. "Look at that—kids from all over wearing those Brooklyn blue caps. October always gets me thinking about baseball, you know? World Series time and all."

Ivy, the younger sister with her hair in braids, laughed. "Our grandfather would love this conversation. He never stops talking about old baseball."

Ben glanced up at the hotel's ornate facade, then back at his customers. "Been watching baseball my whole life, studied every great player you can imagine—Ruth, DiMaggio, Mantle, all the legends. But you know what? None of them, not even the Bambino himself, had the same impact that Jackie Robinson did."

The visitor raised an eyebrow. "That's quite a statement. I mean, the guy was good, but there were bigger stars, right?"

Juniper tilted her head thoughtfully. "We just finished reading his autobiography for my history seminar. The professor made it required reading."

"Smart professor," Ben said, handing over the hot dogs with a knowing smile. "See, that's where most people get it wrong. It wasn't about being the biggest star. Hell, Jackie wasn't even the best player in the Negro Leagues when Branch Rickey picked him in '45." He leaned against his cart, warming to his subject. "You want to know why Robinson was different? Why his impact was so huge?"

"I'm listening," the visitor said, taking a bite.

Ivy jumped in, "Our professor said something about how he was chosen specifically because of his character?"

"Exactly right, young lady. Preparation, my friend," Ben said, gesturing with his tongs. "That was everything with Jackie. Rickey didn't choose him because of pure talent—he chose him because the man was ready in every way that mattered. College educated from UCLA, served as an officer in the Army, understood exactly what he was signing up for. When Robinson stepped onto Ebbets Field in '47, he knew he wasn't just playing baseball. He was representing an entire race of people who'd been shut out of America's pastime."

Ben's eyes grew distant, as if he could see that historic day playing out in front of him. "And man, did they test him. Fans screaming racial slurs, opposing players sliding into him with their spikes high, pitchers throwing at his head. But here's the thing—Rickey had prepared him for all of it. Made him promise to turn the other cheek for three years, no matter what they did to him."

"That must have been brutal," the visitor observed.

Juniper frowned, setting down her hot dog. "I don't know if I could have done that. Just taking abuse and not fighting back? It seems like it would eat you alive inside."

"Nearly broke him, from what I've read," Ben acknowledged. "But you know what Jackie learned? That dignity was his most powerful weapon. Remember that famous moment when Pee Wee Reese put his arm around Robinson's shoulder during a game in Cincinnati? That didn't happen because Jackie fought his way to respect. It happened because he earned it by showing up every day, playing the game right, maintaining his dignity in the face of pure hatred."

Ivy spoke up quietly, "So sometimes the strongest thing you can do is not react?"

"Precisely," Ben said, pointing at her. "You're getting it. But here's the real lesson—and this is advice I think Jackie would give to any young person today trying to make it in life." He looked directly at the two sisters. "When you break a barrier, you're not just opening a door for yourself. You're opening it for everyone who comes behind you. Every time Robinson stole home, every clutch hit, every brilliant play—he wasn't just playing for the Brooklyn Dodgers. He was playing for Willie Mays, for Hank Aaron, for every young black ballplayer who would follow."

Juniper exchanged a glance with her sister. "That's actually really relevant. Juni's applying to medical school," Ivy explained. "She'll be the first in our family to be a doctor."

"Then you understand the weight of it," Ben said to Juniper. "That's a heavy burden."

"It is," Juniper admitted. "Sometimes I feel like I'm carrying my whole family's hopes on my shoulders. Like if I fail, I'm not just failing myself."

"Exactly! But also a privilege, because it means your life has purpose beyond your own success. Robinson understood that. So did Larry Doby, who integrated the American League just months later. They knew failure wasn't just personal—it would set back the cause for who knows how long."

Ben paused to serve another customer, then continued while wiping down his cart. "Now, here's where it gets interesting, and where I think Jackie's real wisdom shows. He turned that other cheek for three years like he promised Rickey. But after 1949? Man started speaking his mind. Disagreed with something? He said so. Saw injustice? Called it out. That's the third lesson—choose your battles wisely. You can't spend your whole life swallowing your pride, but you need to earn the right to speak by proving yourself first."

"Smart strategy," the visitor agreed.

Ivy looked up from her hot dog. "So you're saying Juniper should just take whatever comes at her in medical school until she proves herself?"

"Not exactly," Ben said carefully. "I'm saying she should understand the game she's playing. If someone questions whether she belongs there, she proves them wrong by being the best student in that class. But if someone crosses a line—discriminates, harasses, treats her unjustly—then she speaks up, but strategically. Jackie knew the difference between petty insults and real injustice worth fighting."

Juniper nodded slowly, absorbing this. "That makes sense. My advisor basically told me the same thing last week."

"Oh, he was smart alright," Ben continued. "After his playing days, Robinson carried those lessons into business and civil rights work. When he became an executive with Chock full o' Nuts, he made sure they hired black employees in positions where they could advance. Used his platform from baseball to fight for voting rights and equal opportunity. See, education mattered more to him than raw talent. He was blessed with athletic ability, sure, but what sustained him through the difficult times was his mind. At UCLA, he learned to think critically, express himself clearly, understand that sports was just one part of a larger life."

"That's why our professor assigned his book," Juniper said. "She said his education was the foundation for everything else."

The visitor checked his watch but seemed reluctant to leave. "What else would Robinson tell young people?"

Ben's expression grew more serious. "Don't be afraid to be different. When Jackie played, people criticized his aggressive style—stealing home, taking extra bases, getting in opponents' heads. Said he was too flashy, too bold for a black player. But that aggressive style was part of who he was, and suppressing it would have made him less effective. Be excellent at whatever you choose to do, but be excellent in your own way."

Ivy perked up at this. "I'm an artist," she said. "Everyone keeps telling me to be more commercial, more mainstream. But that's not what I want to create."

"Then don't," Ben said firmly. "Robinson could have played it safe, been just another player. But he changed the game by being himself. You two," he gestured at both sisters, "you're at that age where everyone's got opinions about what you should do with your lives. Listen to wisdom, but trust your own path."

A taxi honked nearby, but Ben continued, his voice taking on a more personal tone. "Family matters most, though. And this is where Jackie's story gets really important for young people today. Rachel Robinson was his anchor through everything—the racism, the pressure, the public scrutiny. She understood the mission they were on together. Building a strong family isn't easy when you're fighting public battles, but it's essential."

Juniper reached over and squeezed her sister's hand. "We've always had each other's backs."

"Hold onto that," Ben said seriously. "Because here's the thing—even great men make mistakes. If I had to guess what Jackie's biggest regret was—and this is something I think about a lot, having raised kids myself—it would be not being present enough for his family during those crucial years. His son Jackie Jr. struggled with the burden of being Jackie Robinson's son, of living up to a name that meant so much to so many people. While Jackie Sr. was out fighting battles for civil rights and social justice, his boy was fighting his own battles with drugs, with identity, with pressure."

The mood at the cart grew somber. Ivy spoke softly, "We didn't learn about that part in school."

"Most people don't talk about it," Ben said. "They lost Jackie Jr. in a car accident in '71. The kid had overcome his addiction, found his way, was working to help other young people. But those crucial teenage years when he needed his father most? Jackie Sr. was often somewhere else, fighting other people's battles instead of being home."

Juniper set down her napkin. "So what you're saying is... I need to succeed in medical school, but not at the expense of the people I love?"

"Exactly," Ben said, his voice warm with approval. "That's the hardest lesson I think Jackie would pass on. Success in the public arena means nothing if you fail your own family. Young people today, especially those thrust into the spotlight, need to remember that the people who love you matter more than the people who applaud you."

"That's heavy," the visitor said softly.

"It is. But that's what made Robinson's impact so much bigger than baseball statistics. He broke down barriers, fought for what was right, but he also learned the cost of those battles. If he could turn back time, I bet he'd find a way to be both the public figure the movement needed and the father his son deserved."

Ivy pulled out her phone and began typing notes. "I want to remember all of this."

Ben smiled at her. "Smart girl. The civil rights movement needed Jackie Robinson the baseball player and public figure. But Jackie Jr. needed Jackie Robinson the father, and too often, he didn't get enough of him."

The visitor extended his hand. "I'm Noah, by the way. From Los Angeles. That was... enlightening."

"Ben. Been slinging dogs and talking baseball on this corner since the Carter administration." They shook hands.

Juniper stepped forward. "Thank you for this, Ben. Really. I feel like I understand him—and what I'm about to face—so much better now."

"That's why I tell these stories," Ben said. "You know what I think Jackie would tell young people as his final piece of advice?"

"What's that?" all three customers asked in unison.

"Stand up for what's right, even when it's costly. Robinson criticized Malcolm X's separatist approach and lost support from some in the black community. Endorsed Nixon in 1960 and faced different criticism. Spoke out against Vietnam and faced even more critics. But he always tried to speak his conscience, not what was politically convenient."

Noah nodded slowly. "So his advice would be to stay true to yourself, fight for others, but don't forget the people closest to you."

"Exactly," Ben said. He turned to Juniper and Ivy. "And you two—remember this when you're out there making your mark. Young people today have opportunities Jackie's generation could never imagine, but they also face challenges he didn't. Greater temptations, more distractions. His advice would be to stay focused on what really matters: family, education, service to others, and never forgetting where you came from."

Ivy finished her hot dog and pulled out her wallet. "How much do we owe you, Ben?"

"First one's on the house for students," he said with a wink. "Consider it an investment in the future."

As Noah turned to walk toward the hotel and the sisters started to leave, Ben called out, "Hey, one more thing Robinson would say—take care of your family first. Everything else, no matter how important it seems, is secondary."

Juniper and Ivy both turned back, and Juniper spoke for both of them. "We will. And thank you—for the hot dogs and for the wisdom."

Noah paused and looked back. "Thanks, Ben. That hot dog was good, but the conversation was better."

"Anytime, friends. That's what this corner's for—good food and better stories."

As the three of them walked away together—Noah toward the Plaza Hotel, and Juniper and Ivy arm in arm toward the subway—Ben smiled and began preparing for the evening rush. Thirty years on this corner had taught him that sometimes the best conversations happened over the simplest meals, and the greatest wisdom often came from understanding both the triumphs and failures of those who came before.

Jackie Robinson had been both hero and human, and his legacy lived not just in the record books, but in the lessons he'd learned along the way—lessons worth sharing with anyone willing to listen. And today, he'd shared those lessons with three people who really needed to hear them: a visitor from California, and two young sisters standing on the edge of their own journey, ready to break their own barriers, carrying Jackie's wisdom forward into a new generation.

Admiral Chester W. Nimitz

Fleet Admiral Chester W. Nimitz was a Texas-born naval officer who served as Commander in Chief of the U.S. Pacific Fleet during World War II, leading Allied forces to victory over Japan across the Pacific theater from the aftermath of Pearl Harbor through the surrender ceremony aboard the USS Missouri in Tokyo Bay.

Finding Your Bearing

Airman Keaton clutched his seabag tighter as he navigated another identical-looking passageway aboard the USS Nimitz. The massive carrier seemed like a floating city compared to the farm in Nebraska where he'd grown up, and every corridor looked the same to his untrained eye. He'd been wandering for twenty minutes trying to find his temporary berthing, and the weight of his gear was starting to make his shoulders ache.

"You look lost, farm boy," came a voice from behind him.

Keaton turned to see Petty Officer First Class Ezra approaching, his dungarees bearing the familiar VA-205 squadron patch. Ezra had the easy confidence of someone who knew exactly where he was going.

"Ezra," Keaton said, shifting his seabag. "Yeah, I'm trying to find compartment 03-95-2-L. Been walking in circles for the better part of an hour."

Ezra chuckled. "Follow me, Keaton. That's down three decks and aft. You were heading forward." As they walked, Ezra navigated the maze of passageways with practiced ease. "First time on the Nimitz?"

"First time on any carrier," Keaton admitted. "This thing's huge. Back home, our biggest building was the grain elevator."

"She's something else, all right. Ninety-seven thousand tons of floating steel. Named after one hell of a sailor, too."

Keaton nodded absently, more focused on trying to memorize their route than the conversation. They descended a ladder, and Ezra pointed to the frame numbers painted on the bulkhead.

"See these numbers? They'll keep you oriented. Frame numbers increase as you go aft, and the compartment designations tell you exactly where you are if you know how to read them."

"Got it," Keaton said, though he wasn't entirely sure he did.

They continued walking, and Ezra glanced at the fresh-faced airman. "So what do you know about Admiral Nimitz? The guy this ship's named after?"

Keaton shrugged. "Navy admiral, I guess. From World War Two?"

Ezra stopped walking and stared at him. "That's it? That's all you know?"

"Should I know more?"

"Jesus, Keaton. You better get up to speed on that subject fast, or you're going to catch hell from every chief and officer on this boat. Especially the old-timers." Ezra resumed walking, but his pace was more measured now. "Look, I've been on this ship three times for workups, and I've learned that knowing about Nimitz isn't just history—it's about understanding what it means to be a sailor."

They reached a junction in the passageway, and Ezra pointed left. "Your compartment's that way, but hold up a minute. Let me tell you what you need to know."

Keaton set his seabag down gratefully and leaned against the bulkhead.

"Chester Nimitz wasn't just any admiral," Ezra began. "He commanded the entire Pacific Fleet during World War Two. Took over right after Pearl Harbor when everything was falling apart. But here's the thing—he didn't start out perfect. Early in his career, he ran a ship aground and got court-martialed for it."

"Court-martialed?" Keaton's eyes widened.

"Yep. But instead of letting it ruin him, he learned from it. His grandfather had told him something when he was young—that the sea is like life itself, a stern taskmaster. The best way to get along with either is to learn all you can, do your best, and don't worry about things you can't control."

Ezra leaned against the opposite bulkhead. "That's lesson number one for you, farm boy. You're going to make mistakes. Hell, we all do. The difference between the sailors who make it and the ones who wash out is how you handle those mistakes. Own up to them, learn from them, and do better next time."

"Makes sense," Keaton said.

"Nimitz also understood something that a lot of people forget—amateurs study tactics, but professionals study logistics. You know what that means for you as an AZ?"

Keaton thought about it. "That keeping the planes flying is just as important as how they're flown?"

"Now you're getting it. The glamorous stuff—the flying, the combat—that's what makes the headlines. But it's the maintainers, the supply folks, the people who keep everything running that actually win wars. Don't ever let anyone make you feel like your job isn't crucial."

A group of sailors walked past, and Ezra nodded to them before continuing. "But here's something else Nimitz knew—your technical skills aren't enough. You've got to understand the bigger picture. Every decision you make, even as an E-3, affects other people. Maybe it's the pilot who flies the plane you worked on, maybe it's the sailor working the next shift who has to deal with what you left behind."

"I never thought about it that way."

"Most people don't, especially when they're starting out. But Nimitz said the best leaders think not just about 'Will this work?' but 'What precedent does this set?' You might just be fixing hydraulic systems now, but someday you might be a chief responsible for a whole shop. Start thinking like a leader now."

They picked up the seabag and continued toward Keaton's compartment. "There's something else," Ezra said as they walked. "Nimitz spent a lot of time in submarines early in his career. You know what he learned there?"

"What?"

"That in tight spaces, under pressure, your real character shows. There's no hiding behind rank or bullshit when you're packed into a submarine, and there's no hiding on a carrier either. People figure out real quick whether you know what you're doing and whether they can trust you."

They stopped in front of a door marked with the compartment number Keaton had been looking for. "This is you," Ezra said. "But before you go in, one more thing. Nimitz always said that true authority doesn't come from rank—it comes from competence you've proven under pressure. People will follow you not because they have to, but because they trust your judgment and believe you care about their welfare."

Keaton nodded, feeling the weight of the advice.

"And one last thing," Ezra added, his tone becoming more serious. "Nimitz later said that if he could change one thing about his life, he would have spent more time with his family. The Navy's going to demand a lot from you, especially if you make it a career. Don't forget that there's life outside these bulkheads. Success in the Navy means nothing if you lose the people who matter most."

"Thanks, Ezra. I really appreciate the guidance."

"Don't mention it. Just remember—you're not just representing yourself on this ship. You're representing VA-205, and in a way, you're carrying on the tradition that Admiral Nimitz helped build. Make it count."

As Ezra walked away, Keaton opened the door to his compartment. Inside, he found a dozen other sailors already settling in, their gear stowed with military precision. An older petty officer looked up from his rack.

"You Keaton? VA-205?"

"Yes, Petty Officer."

"Good. Stow your gear in that rack there. And son?" The petty officer's expression was serious. "Welcome aboard the Nimitz. This ship has a reputation to maintain. See that you help us keep it."

As Keaton began unpacking his seabag, he found himself thinking about what Ezra had told him. Learn all you can, do your best, don't worry about what you can't control. Own your mistakes. Think about the bigger picture. Take care of the people around you. It seemed like simple advice, but somehow Keaton sensed that living up to it would be anything but simple. Outside the porthole, he could see the vast expanse of the Pacific, the same ocean where Admiral Nimitz had faced his greatest challenges. Now it was Keaton's turn to see what kind of sailor he would become.

He folded his civilian clothes and placed them in his rack locker, symbolically putting his farm boy past behind him. Whatever lay ahead during these two weeks of carrier qualifications, he was determined to prove himself worthy of serving aboard a ship that bore the name of such a remarkable leader. The sea was indeed a stern taskmaster, but Keaton was ready to learn.

President Thomas Jefferson

Thomas Jefferson was the third President of the United States and primary author of the Declaration of Independence, a brilliant polymath who championed individual liberty, limited government, and public education while embodying the contradictions of his era through his ownership of enslaved people despite proclaiming that "all men are created equal."

The Art of Disagreement

The afternoon sun cast long shadows across the Tidal Basin as Kat, TJ, Sabrina, and Virginia emerged from the Jefferson Memorial, their footsteps echoing on the marble steps. Kat shook her head as she looked back at the towering bronze statue.

"It's impressive architecture, I'll give you that," she said, adjusting her sunglasses, "but I find it a bit unsettling that we still treat Jefferson like some oracle of wisdom. His ideas about small government and individual liberty might have worked in the 1700s, but we're living in a completely different world."

TJ paused at the bottom of the steps, genuinely puzzled. "What do you mean? I think his core principles are more relevant than ever."

Sabrina, who had been quiet until now, jumped in. "I'm with Kat on this one. As someone who studies economic policy, I can tell you that Jefferson's agrarian vision is completely obsolete. He couldn't have imagined multinational corporations, digital currencies, or the gig economy."

Virginia laughed and adjusted her backpack. "But that's exactly why we should study him. I'm a history teacher, and what I try to get my students to understand is that it's not about applying his solutions—it's about understanding his method of thinking."

"Think about it, TJ." Kat gestured broadly toward the city around them. "Jefferson lived in a world of three million people, mostly farmers, no corporations, no global economy, no climate change, no internet. His whole vision of minimal government worked when communities were small and self-sufficient. But today? We need robust federal programs, environmental regulations, social safety nets. His 'that government is best which governs least' philosophy would be a disaster in our complex, interconnected world."

They began walking along the path that circled the memorial, tourists streaming past them in both directions. TJ considered her argument as they walked. "But I think you're missing what made Jefferson really brilliant. He wasn't just about small government for its own sake—he was about questioning authority and adapting institutions to serve human flourishing. Remember, this was a guy who told people to never stop questioning authority, including the authority of previous generations."

"That's a nice sentiment," Kat replied, "but it's easy to say 'question authority' when you're part of the ruling class. The man owned slaves while writing about liberty. He had no concept of modern economics, technology, or social issues. What could an 18th-century plantation owner possibly tell us about managing a 21st-century society?"

Virginia stopped walking and turned to face the group. "Actually, Kat, that's where I think you're being unfair. Yes, Jefferson's moral failure on slavery is indefensible. But dismissing everything he thought because he lived in the 1700s is like saying we shouldn't study ancient philosophy because the Greeks didn't have smartphones."

Sabrina nodded thoughtfully. "Virginia has a point. I mean, we still teach Adam Smith's economic theories even though he wrote before the Industrial Revolution. The question is whether the underlying principles have value, not whether the specific applications are outdated."

A group of school children ran past them, their teacher calling after them to stay together. TJ watched them for a moment before responding. "You know what I think Jefferson would focus on if he were alive today? Education. He spent his final years founding the University of Virginia because he believed that democracy only works if citizens are educated enough to make informed decisions. Isn't that exactly what we're struggling with now—how to have an informed electorate in an age of misinformation?"

"Now that," Virginia said emphatically, "is something I see every day in my classroom. Kids have access to infinite information but no framework for evaluating it. Jefferson's emphasis on critical thinking and civic education is desperately needed."

Kat had to admit that struck a chord. "Okay, the education focus is valid. But TJ, you're basically creating a modern Jefferson in your head. The real Jefferson's wisdom was limited by his time and circumstances."

"Was it though?" TJ stopped walking and turned to face her. "Think about what he learned from watching the French Revolution. He saw how revolutionary ideals could turn into mob violence and concluded that lasting change had to be built on education and enlightenment, not just passion and grievance. Doesn't that sound exactly like what we need to understand about social movements today?"

Sabrina interjected, "That's actually a really important observation for economic transitions too. You can't just tear down existing systems without having educated people ready to build something better. We see this in developing nations all the time—rapid change without institutional capacity leads to chaos."

They had reached a bench overlooking the water, and Kat sat down, still skeptical but intrigued despite herself. Virginia and Sabrina settled on either side of her, with TJ leaning against a nearby railing.

"I'll grant you that observation about sustainable change," Kat said. "But what about his biggest moral failure? He compromised on slavery his entire life for political expediency. What makes you think he wouldn't compromise on climate change or income inequality the same way?"

Virginia spoke up, her voice serious. "As a historian, I have to say—that's the question that keeps me up at night. How do we learn from someone who so spectacularly failed at the most important moral issue of his time?"

TJ watched a paddle boat make its way across the basin before responding. "Actually, I think that failure might be exactly why his wisdom is still relevant. By the end of his life, he was calling slavery 'holding a wolf by the ears'—dangerous to hold, but more dangerous to release without proper preparation. He knew he'd failed to resolve the greatest moral contradiction of his time, and I think that failure taught him something important about the cost of political calculation over moral clarity."

"So you think his regret about slavery would make him more decisive on other moral issues?" Kat asked, genuinely curious now.

Sabrina leaned forward. "There's actually an economic parallel here. Jefferson opposed Hamilton's financial system because he saw how concentrated wealth and power could corrupt democracy. He wasn't wrong about that—we're living through the consequences right now. Income inequality, corporate lobbying, the influence of money in politics. He identified a fundamental tension between capitalism and democracy that we still haven't resolved."

"I think it would make him understand the danger of letting political expedience override fundamental principles," TJ replied. "And speaking of principles, remember his battles with Hamilton over the national bank? Jefferson saw how financial interests could corrupt political institutions when they got too cozy together. Isn't that exactly what we're dealing with today?"

Kat found herself nodding. "The corporate influence in politics thing is definitely relevant. Citizens United would have horrified him."

"Exactly," Virginia added. "And think about his approach to religious liberty. He didn't just want separation of church and state because he was anti-religion—he thought it protected both good government and genuine faith. That framework of protecting individual conscience against institutional pressure seems pretty applicable to contemporary civil rights issues."

A couple walked by holding hands, and Kat watched them before responding. "I suppose the separation principle does extend beyond just religious issues. Personal autonomy, marriage equality, reproductive rights—they all fit under that umbrella of protecting individual conscience."

Sabrina stood and stretched. "You know what fascinates me from an economic perspective? Jefferson's idea that debt was a form of tyranny—that one generation shouldn't be able to bind future generations with financial obligations. Whether you agree with that or not, it's exactly the conversation we should be having about national debt and climate change. We're making decisions now that future generations will pay for."

"That's a powerful point," TJ said, getting more animated. "Jefferson believed that each generation had to adapt the Constitution to new circumstances. He said the earth belongs to the living, not the dead. He literally argued against being bound by the wisdom of previous generations—including his own."

Kat laughed despite herself. "So Jefferson is arguing against Jeffersonianism. That's actually pretty meta."

Virginia grinned. "That's what makes him such a great teaching tool. He contradicts himself constantly, forces students to think rather than just memorize. The worst thing you can do is treat him as an infallible sage."

"Right?" TJ continued. "But think about how that principle applies to something like climate change. Jefferson was obsessed with promoting science and innovation. He thought governments that failed to advance human knowledge were failing their people. If he were alive today, wouldn't he be demanding that we listen to climate scientists and develop new technologies?"

"You're reaching," Kat said, but her tone was more thoughtful than dismissive. "Though I admit, his scientific curiosity was genuine. He really did believe in progress through knowledge."

Sabrina nodded enthusiastically. "And he actually practiced what he preached. He experimented with crop rotation, studied meteorology, collected fossils. He understood that practical knowledge improved people's lives. That's the kind of evidence-based policymaking we need."

TJ leaned forward, warming to his theme. "And consider his foreign policy insights. He spent years in France, saw how European solutions didn't necessarily work in American contexts. He believed in learning from other nations but adapting their lessons to your own circumstances. That sounds like exactly the kind of nuanced thinking we need for international cooperation on global challenges."

Virginia added, "That's something I try to teach my students—context matters. You can't just copy-paste solutions from one culture or time period to another. You have to understand the principles and adapt them."

Kat stood up and began walking again, the others falling into step beside her. "Okay, I'm starting to see your point about principles versus specific policies. But here's what still bothers me—even if his intellectual framework was sound, the man himself made terrible compromises when it mattered most. He prioritized political unity over moral clarity on slavery. Why should we expect he'd be any braver on contemporary issues?"

They had completed their circuit of the memorial and were approaching the steps again. TJ thought carefully before responding. "Maybe because by the end of his life, he understood the cost of those compromises. He wrote about wishing he'd acted more boldly, about how his generation's failure to resolve slavery was becoming a heavier burden for future generations. That kind of self-awareness and regret might actually make someone more likely to act decisively when faced with the next great moral crisis."

"That's... actually a compelling argument," Kat admitted reluctantly. "The idea that learning from moral failure could lead to moral courage."

Virginia spoke quietly. "In my classes, I don't present Jefferson as a hero or a villain. I present him as someone who was brilliant and flawed, someone whose ideas outlasted his personal failures. The question isn't whether we should venerate him—it's whether we can learn from both his insights and his mistakes."

"And think about how he maintained his friendship with John Adams despite their bitter political differences," TJ added. "They spent years as political enemies, then reconciled in old age and corresponded until they died. Jefferson understood that you could have fundamental disagreements with someone and still respect their patriotism and good faith. We've completely lost that capacity."

Kat nodded vigorously. "God, yes. Everything is existential conflict now. You can't even disagree on tax policy without questioning someone's basic decency."

Sabrina sighed. "In economics, we're supposed to be able to debate different approaches to the same problem. But now every policy disagreement becomes a moral judgment. Jefferson and Hamilton hated each other's visions for America, but they both wanted America to succeed."

"Jefferson worried about that too—about partisan newspapers that prioritized sensation over truth, division over unity," TJ said. "He thought citizens needed to learn to distinguish between honest disagreement and malicious misrepresentation. Sound familiar?"

"Social media has made that problem exponentially worse," Kat agreed. "Though I notice he managed to maintain personal relationships across political divides. That seems almost impossible now."

They had reached TJ's car, but no one moved to get in. The conversation had taken on a momentum of its own. "You know what really strikes me about Jefferson," TJ said, leaning against the car, "is how he ended his life. He could have retired to Monticello and enjoyed his reputation, but instead he spent his final years founding a university, trying to shape the next generation of citizen-leaders. He really believed that democracy required active, ongoing participation from educated citizens."

Virginia's eyes lit up. "Yes! That's what I wish more people understood. He saw education as the foundation of democracy, not just a personal benefit. Every citizen needed to be equipped to participate meaningfully in self-governance."

Kat considered this. "The civic engagement angle is hard to argue with. He did see citizenship as a responsibility, not just a privilege."

"Exactly," Sabrina added. "And from an economic standpoint, an educated citizenry makes better collective decisions. Democracies with higher education levels tend to have more stable economies and less corruption."

"He understood that freedom isn't something you achieve once and then coast on," TJ continued. "He talked about how each generation had to earn and maintain liberty through active participation. The tree of liberty doesn't just need occasional dramatic refreshing—it needs constant tending by people who understand their civic duties."

Kat finally opened the car door but didn't get in. "I hate to admit it, but you three have actually changed my mind somewhat. Not about idealizing Jefferson—I still think that's dangerous—but about the value of engaging seriously with his intellectual framework."

"What convinced you?" Virginia asked, genuinely curious.

"I think it was the point about learning from moral failure," Kat replied. "The idea that his regret over slavery might actually make his approach to other moral issues more valuable, not less. And the civic engagement stuff—we really have lost that sense of citizenship as active responsibility."

Sabrina smiled. "For me, it's always been about the questions he asked rather than the answers he gave. How do we balance liberty and order? How do we prevent concentrated power from corrupting democracy? How do we educate citizens for self-governance? Those questions are timeless."

TJ opened the driver's side door. "So you think his wisdom might be relevant after all?"

Kat buckled her seatbelt and thought for a moment. "I think his approach to thinking about problems—questioning authority, promoting education, adapting to new circumstances, maintaining civic relationships across disagreements—those intellectual habits might be timeless, even if his specific 18th-century solutions aren't."

Virginia, settling into the backseat, added, "And maybe that's the lesson. We don't need Jefferson the person or Jefferson the politician. We need Jefferson the critical thinker, Jefferson the questioner, Jefferson the believer in human capacity for growth."

"Just not Jefferson the slaveholder," Sabrina said from beside her. "We can acknowledge his intellectual contributions without excusing his moral failures."

"Obviously," everyone agreed in unison, then laughed at the synchronicity.

As they drove away from the memorial, Kat found herself wondering what Jefferson would make of their conversation. Would he be pleased that four citizens were actively grappling with questions of governance and liberty, or dismayed that they were still working through problems he'd hoped his generation would solve?

Perhaps, she thought as the memorial disappeared in the side mirror, he'd appreciate that they were at least asking the right questions—and that they'd managed to disagree respectfully while searching for truth together. Maybe that was the most Jeffersonian thing of all.

From the backseat, Virginia voiced what everyone was thinking: "You know what? We should do this more often. Not just visit monuments, but actually talk about these ideas. Really engage with them."

"Without social media turning it into a screaming match," Sabrina added with a laugh.

"Now that," TJ said, glancing in the rearview mirror, "would be something Jefferson would definitely approve of."

Amelia Earhart

Amelia Earhart (1897-1937) was a pioneering American aviator who became the first woman to fly solo across the Atlantic Ocean and set numerous aviation records before mysteriously disappearing over the Pacific Ocean during her attempt to circumnavigate the globe.

Breaking Barriers

The thunderous roar of F/A-18 Super Hornets split the azure Virginia sky as Admiral Elana and Dr. Kevin stood on the observation deck at Naval Air Station Oceana. Below them, the sprawling base stretched across nearly 6,000 acres of Tidewater landscape, its four runways forming precise geometric lines against the coastal plain. The smell of jet fuel mixed with salt air from the nearby Atlantic, while thousands of spectators filled the bleachers for the annual Oceana Air Show.

"Magnificent, isn't it?" Admiral Elana gestured toward a formation of Blue Angels banking sharply over the crowd. "Seventy years of naval aviation excellence, right here at the Navy's Master Jet Base."

Dr. Kevin, the Smithsonian's curator of aeronautical history, adjusted his glasses as he watched the precision flying. "Indeed. Though I'd argue we're standing on the shoulders of pioneers who never got to see jets break the sound barrier."

"Ah, you're thinking of Earhart again." Elana's tone carried a note of friendly skepticism. "Kevin, I respect your passion for aviation history, but let's be honest—what did Amelia Earhart actually contribute beyond publicity stunts?"

The two had debated this topic before, most recently at a symposium on aviation pioneers. Kevin turned from the aerial display, his expression earnest. "Elana, that's exactly the kind of thinking that would have kept half our potential pilots grounded forever."

A squadron of F-35C Lightning IIs streaked overhead, their engines creating a wall of sound that momentarily paused their conversation. In the distance, the distinctive silhouette of Oceana's control tower rose against gathering clouds, coordinating the carefully choreographed dance of military and civilian aircraft.

"Look," Elana continued as the noise subsided, "I command one of the largest naval air stations in the world. I've got over 17,000 personnel here, operating the most sophisticated aircraft ever built. We're talking about combat readiness, technological advancement, strategic capability. What does a 1930s publicity seeker have to do with any of that?"

Kevin smiled, knowing his old friend was deliberately provocative. They'd served together years ago before their careers diverged—hers toward command, his toward academia. "You're missing the forest for the trees, Admiral. Earhart didn't just fly airplanes; she broke barriers that made everything you see here possible."

"How so?"

"Think about what aviation was in her era. An exclusive boys' club where women were considered incapable of handling the physical and mental demands of flight. Every time she climbed into a cockpit, she was proving that capability had nothing to do with gender. Do you think you'd be commanding this base today if someone hadn't first challenged those assumptions?"

A formation of vintage warbirds—a P-51 Mustang, an F4U Corsair, and a TBM Avenger—passed overhead in a heritage flight, their propeller-driven engines a stark contrast to the jets. The crowd below erupted in cheers, many recognizing the historical significance of the aircraft.

Elana watched the vintage planes thoughtfully. "Point taken. But breaking social barriers is different from advancing aviation itself."

"Is it, though?" Kevin pulled out his phone, scrolling to a photo from the Naval Academy's recent graduation. "Thirty-seven percent of this year's pilot candidates were women. That pipeline exists because someone proved it was possible. And it wasn't just about gender—Earhart understood that aviation's future depended on expanding the pool of talent, not restricting it."

The afternoon sun glinted off the glass facade of Oceana's state-of-the-art training facilities. Inside those buildings, the next generation of naval aviators learned everything from basic flight principles to advanced electronic warfare—a far cry from the simple instruments Earhart had relied upon during her trans-Atlantic crossings.

"But what about the technical contributions?" Elana pressed. "The records, the routes, the actual advancement of aviation science?"

"That's where you're underestimating her impact." Kevin gestured toward the busy flight line where maintenance crews swarmed over aircraft between demonstrations. "Every long-range flight she attempted generated data—weather patterns, fuel consumption, radio communications, navigation techniques. She was essentially conducting research flights that pushed the boundaries of what was known about aviation endurance and reliability."

A massive C-130 Hercules lumbered past the tower, its four turboprop engines and high-wing design a testament to decades of evolution in aircraft engineering. The plane's utilitarian appearance contrasted sharply with the sleek fighters, yet both represented crucial advances in their respective fields.

"Think about her preparation methodology," Kevin continued. "Meticulous planning combined with the ability to adapt when conditions changed. Sound familiar? That's the same mindset we train into every pilot who graduates from Pensacola."

Elana nodded slowly. "The preparation I'll grant you. But the risks she took—flying into weather systems, attempting routes with minimal backup plans—that's exactly what we train our pilots to avoid."

"True, but someone had to take those risks to establish the baseline knowledge we now take for granted. You can't develop safety protocols without understanding what the dangerous variables are."

An F-22 Raptor screamed overhead in a high-speed pass, its angular stealth design representing the pinnacle of fighter aircraft technology. The crowd fell silent for a moment, awed by the raw power and sophistication of the machine.

"You know what I think Earhart would say if she could see all this?" Kevin asked, watching the fighter disappear into the distance.

"Enlighten me."

"She'd say the technology is magnificent, but she'd be more interested in who's flying it. She'd want to know if we're still telling people their dreams are too big, if we're still creating artificial barriers based on background or circumstances. She'd ask whether we're using these incredible capabilities to connect people or divide them."

Elana considered this as another group of aircraft took to the sky—a mixed formation of international aircraft participating in the show, including planes from allied nations. "She'd probably be amazed that aviation has become so routine that people travel across oceans for business meetings."

"And concerned that we've maybe lost some of the wonder," Kevin added. "She wrote once about seeing the curvature of the earth from altitude, about understanding both how large and small our planet really is. I think she'd worry that we're so focused on getting from point A to point B that we've forgotten the perspective that flight can provide."

The air show's grand finale was beginning—a massive formation flight involving dozens of aircraft from different eras and nations. The sight was spectacular against the backdrop of Virginia Beach's coastline, where the Chesapeake Bay met the Atlantic Ocean.

"What would she advise young people today?" Elana asked, genuinely curious now.

Kevin thought for a moment, watching a young girl in the crowd point excitedly at the flying display. "I think she'd tell them to find their own horizon—whether that's in aviation, technology, medicine, or any other field. She'd say that the barriers they face aren't permanent structures but temporary obstacles that can be overcome with preparation, persistence, and the willingness to support others along the way."

"And she'd probably tell them to fail better," Elana added with a slight smile.

"Exactly. She understood that every failure teaches you something essential about success. The key is being prepared enough that failure doesn't cost you everything."

As the formation flights concluded and the crowd began to disperse, the two friends remained on the observation deck. Below them, Oceana continued its operations—fighters returning from training missions, cargo planes delivering supplies, the constant rhythm of one of America's busiest naval air facilities.

"You know what strikes me most about this place?" Elana said finally. "It's not just the technology or the capability. It's the fact that we have people from every conceivable background learning to fly some of the most sophisticated machines ever built. Farm kids from Iowa, inner-city kids from Detroit, immigrants' children, people who fifty years ago wouldn't have been allowed near a military cockpit."

"That's Earhart's real legacy," Kevin agreed.

Albert Einstein

Albert Einstein was a German-born theoretical physicist who revolutionized our understanding of space, time, and gravity through his theories of special and general relativity, won the Nobel Prize in Physics in 1921 for his explanation of the photoelectric effect, and became one of history's most influential scientists while also advocating for civil rights and world peace.

Relatively Speaking

Dr. Haylee set her mug down on the scratched wooden table as her colleague Dr. Tom slumped into the chair across from her. The late afternoon sun streamed through the university's physics building windows, casting long shadows across stacks of journal articles and abandoned coffee cups.

"I just came from the undergraduate seminar," Tom said, shaking his head. "Half the students think Einstein is some kind of ancient relic. One kid actually asked if we still 'believe in' relativity, like it's some outdated philosophy."

Haylee raised an eyebrow. "And you disagree?"

"Of course I disagree! But honestly, Haylee, sometimes I wonder if we're clinging to the past. Einstein died seventy years ago. We've got quantum computers, CRISPR, artificial intelligence that can write poetry. Maybe it's time to admit that a patent clerk from the early 1900s doesn't have much to teach us about navigating the 21st century."

Haylee leaned back, a slight smile playing at her lips. "That's exactly the kind of thinking Einstein would have warned us about."

"Oh, come on," Tom groaned. "Don't tell me you're going to quote 'imagination is more important than knowledge' at me."

"No, though that's actually profound advice for our current moment." Haylee paused, organizing her thoughts. "Think about it, Tom. We're living through an era where people are demanding blind obedience to algorithms, to social media feeds, to whatever authority figure shouts the loudest. Einstein fled Nazi Germany precisely because he understood what happens when brilliant minds stop thinking for themselves. That lesson isn't outdated—it's more urgent than ever."

The coffee room door swung open, and Dr. Jesse walked in, her laptop bag slung over one shoulder. "Sorry, am I interrupting?" she asked, catching the tail end of their conversation.

"Not at all," Haylee said, gesturing to an empty chair. "Tom and I are debating whether Einstein has anything useful to tell us anymore."

Jesse set down her bag and poured herself some water. "Oh, this argument again? Tom, you can't seriously be on the 'Einstein is irrelevant' side."

Tom shifted uncomfortably. "I'm just saying that generic advice about critical thinking isn't particularly special. Any philosopher could have said that."

"Could they?" both Haylee and Jesse said almost simultaneously, then laughed.

Jesse pulled out the chair and sat down. "Einstein wasn't just talking about abstract intellectual freedom. He was a scientist who understood that questioning everything—even your own assumptions—is literally how we discover truth about the universe. When he imagined riding alongside a beam of light, he wasn't following established protocols. He was playing with impossible scenarios, letting his mind wander into territory that conventional thinking said was absurd."

"See, this is exactly what I was saying," Haylee added.

"But we don't need that kind of revolutionary thinking anymore," Tom insisted. "We've got the Standard Model, we understand the fundamental forces—"

"Do we?" Haylee interrupted. "Dark matter, dark energy, the measurement problem in quantum mechanics, the hard problem of consciousness? Tom, we're like explorers who've mapped the coastline and think we understand the ocean. Einstein would tell us that our sense of certainty is precisely what's holding us back."

Jesse nodded vigorously. "And honestly, from my perspective in computational physics, we're seeing exactly this problem. Everyone's so focused on feeding data into neural networks and optimizing algorithms that we've stopped asking the fundamental questions. We're building increasingly sophisticated tools without understanding the deeper principles."

Tom poured more coffee, considering. "Okay, but what about practical issues? Climate change, inequality, political polarization? What could a physicist from 1955 possibly tell us about those problems?"

Haylee's expression grew more serious. "Everything, actually. Einstein spent his later years deeply troubled by what his theories had made possible. He understood that scientific progress without ethical consideration becomes mere cleverness—and cleverness without wisdom can destroy what it seeks to protect. Sound familiar? We've got the technology to solve climate change, but we're paralyzed by short-term thinking and tribal politics."

"So what would his advice be?"

"Stop building walls between people and start building bridges." Haylee gestured toward the window, where students from dozens of countries were crossing the campus quad. "Einstein believed we needed to see ourselves as citizens of the cosmos rather than prisoners of our narrow identities. The fundamental laws of nature don't recognize borders—why should we let artificial categories prevent us from working together on problems that affect everyone?"

Jesse leaned forward, her eyes bright with enthusiasm. "And you know what's fascinating? In my work with international research collaborations, I see this play out every day. When scientists from different countries work together on a problem—really work together, not just exchange emails—the borders dissolve. A physicist in Mumbai and one in Munich both speak the language of mathematics and shared curiosity. Einstein understood that decades before we had the internet."

Tom was quiet for a moment. "I'll grant you that. But surely some of his ideas were products of his time?"

"Absolutely. And he'd be the first to tell us to question them." Haylee leaned forward. "But here's what's timeless: his insistence that wonder and curiosity are the engines of human progress. We're so busy optimizing and quantifying everything that we're losing our sense of awe. When was the last time you just sat quietly and marveled at the fact that consciousness can contemplate its own existence? That seemed impossible until it happened."

"You sound like you're describing meditation," Tom observed.

"Einstein would have loved that connection," Jesse interjected. "I actually read that he used to take long walks and sail alone precisely to create space for deep thinking. He understood that the greatest insights come during quiet moments—sailing alone, walking peaceful streets, sitting in solitude with books and ideas."

"But he also knew that wisdom grows in solitude and flowers in community," Haylee added. "We need both the space to think deeply and the courage to share those thoughts with others who might challenge them."

Tom stared into his coffee. "You know what strikes me? If Einstein were alive today, he'd probably be horrified by how we've weaponized information the way previous generations weaponized atoms."

"Exactly." Haylee's voice grew passionate. "He spent his final years regretting that letter he wrote to Roosevelt about atomic weapons. He realized that good intentions and brilliant theories aren't enough—you have to consider the full human cost of unleashing new powers into the world. Imagine what he'd say about artificial intelligence, genetic engineering, or social media algorithms designed to manipulate behavior."

Jesse's expression turned somber. "I think about this constantly in my field. We're developing AI systems that can predict human behavior, generate convincing misinformation, automate decisions about people's lives. And the whole time, the question isn't 'should we?' but 'how fast can we?' Einstein would be appalled."

"So what would be his advice for handling those technologies?" Tom asked.

"Remember that science serves humanity, not the reverse," Haylee said without hesitation. "Every breakthrough should make us ask not just 'can we do this?' but 'should we do this?' and 'who benefits?' Einstein believed that if we could learn to see the bigger picture—to think like citizens of the cosmos rather than tribal competitors—we might actually solve problems instead of just creating more sophisticated ways to fight about them."

Jesse glanced at her phone, then looked up. "You know, I have to share something. Last week, I was reviewing code for a machine learning project, and I found myself just going through the motions—checking syntax, optimizing functions. Then I stopped and asked myself what Einstein would do. Would he just accept the problem as framed, or would he step back and question the entire approach?"

"And?" Haylee prompted.

"And I realized we were trying to solve the wrong problem entirely. We were so focused on making predictions more accurate that we'd lost sight of whether those predictions were even useful or ethical. Einstein's ghost saved us from wasting six months on something fundamentally misguided."

Tom finished his coffee and stood up slowly. "You know what's funny? I came in here thinking Einstein was irrelevant, but now I'm wondering if we're just not brave enough to follow his example."

"How so?"

"He spent decades trying to develop a unified field theory, failing over and over again, but never giving up on the passionate pursuit of understanding. We get discouraged if our grant applications are rejected or our papers need revisions. Maybe we need to embrace uncertainty and failure as teachers instead of obstacles."

Haylee smiled. "Now you're thinking like Einstein."

Jesse stood up as well, gathering her things. "And maybe that's the real gift he left us—not just his theories, but his approach to life. The courage to question everything, the humility to admit what we don't know, and the persistence to keep searching for truth even when the path seems impossible."

As the three scientists gathered their papers and headed toward the door, Tom paused. "One more thing. If Einstein's advice is so timeless, why do you think people resist it?"

Haylee considered the question carefully. "Because it requires us to change how we see ourselves. It's easier to cling to certainties and tribal identities than to admit we're all just curious children trying to understand an impossibly vast and mysterious universe. Einstein's real challenge isn't scientific—it's spiritual. He's asking us to live with wonder, think with courage, and love with our whole hearts."

Jesse held the door open for them. "My grandmother used to say that the hardest journey is from the head to the heart. Einstein made that journey—from pure mathematics to passionate advocacy for humanity. Maybe that's why his example still matters."

The three scientists walked out into the fading afternoon light, their conversation echoing in the empty coffee room where countless similar discussions had taken place over the decades—the timeless human struggle to balance knowledge with wisdom, progress with responsibility, and individual insight with collective understanding.

Mahatma Gandhi

Mahatma Gandhi was an Indian lawyer and political leader who pioneered non-violent civil disobedience as a means of resistance, led India's independence movement against British colonial rule through methods including fasts, protests, and the famous Salt March, and became a global symbol of peace and social justice before his assassination in New Delhi.

Seeing and Being Seen

Amanda adjusted the banner one more time, checking that the corners were securely tied to the metal posts. Around her, Liberty Park was slowly filling with people carrying signs reading "Housing is a Human Right" and "No One Sleeps Outside." The late afternoon sun cast long shadows across the grass where their permitted demonstration would begin in thirty minutes.

"Good turnout," said Jon, approaching with a clipboard and a box of flyers. He'd been her co-organizer for three months now, ever since the city had announced plans to clear the encampment under the highway overpass without providing alternative housing.

"Better than I expected," Amanda replied, watching a group of college students unfurl a large banner. "Though I'm worried about what happens after everyone goes home tonight. Another rally, another feel-good moment, and then what? The people sleeping rough are still sleeping rough."

Jon set down his clipboard and looked at her. "You sound like you're having second thoughts about today."

"Not second thoughts, exactly. It's just..." Amanda gestured toward the gathering crowd. "Sometimes I wonder if we're just performing our own righteousness instead of actually solving anything. Like, what would Gandhi do in this situation?"

"Gandhi?" Jon looked skeptical. "Amanda, we're dealing with a housing crisis in a major American city in 2025. What's a guy who died almost eighty years ago going to teach us about homelessness policy?"

"I've been reading about him lately," Amanda said, pulling out her phone to silence it. "And I keep thinking about how he always insisted that you have to be the change you want to see. Like, how many of us here today have actually invited someone experiencing homelessness into our own homes?"

Jon frowned. "That's not really practical, though. We need systemic solutions---more funding for affordable housing, mental health services, addiction treatment. Individual charity isn't going to solve a structural problem."

"I'm not talking about charity," Amanda said, her voice gaining intensity. "I'm talking about authenticity. If we're demanding that the city treat homeless people with dignity, are we actually treating them with dignity ourselves? Or are we just marching about them without really including them?"

"We have speakers from the homeless community," Jon pointed out. "Three of them."

"Three out of fifty speakers. And how many of us actually know their names, their stories?" Amanda watched as a man pushing a shopping cart full of belongings walked along the park's edge, giving their gathering a wide berth. "Gandhi spent years living among the poorest people in India. He cleaned latrines, he lived in the slums. He said you can't serve people from a distance."

Jon shook his head. "That's exactly the kind of thinking that keeps people stuck in poverty tourism instead of actually changing policy. We don't need to live in tents to advocate for housing policy."

"But maybe we need to understand what it actually feels like," Amanda countered. "Gandhi would probably say that if we want politicians to see homeless people as fully human, we need to see them as fully human ourselves. Not as a cause to rally around, but as neighbors, as teachers."

"Teachers?" Jon's voice carried a note of irritation. "Amanda, these are people in crisis. They need help, not romanticization."

"That's not what I mean." Amanda sat down on a nearby bench, and Jon joined her reluctantly. "I was talking to this woman, Sarah, who's been sleeping in her car for eight months. She told me that the hardest part isn't the cold or the hunger---it's being invisible. People look right through her, like she's not even there. And I realized that even in our activism, we sometimes do the same thing. We talk about 'the homeless' as a category instead of talking with actual people."

Jon was quiet for a moment, watching their volunteers hand out flyers to passersby. "Okay, I can see that. But what's the alternative? We can't solve everyone's individual problems."

"Gandhi would probably say that's exactly backwards," Amanda said. "He'd say that trying to solve the problem without transforming ourselves is like trying to clean a mirror with dirty hands. He spent time spinning cotton every day, not because India needed more thread, but because he needed to understand dignity in simple work, self-reliance, what it meant to provide for basic needs."

"So what, we should all start spinning wheels?"

Amanda laughed despite herself. "No, but maybe we should ask harder questions about our own relationship to consumption, to housing, to community. Like, why do we think it's normal for some people to have multiple homes while others have none? Gandhi lived with almost nothing and said he'd never been happier."

"That's fine for him, but---"

"No, wait," Amanda interrupted. "I'm not saying we should all become ascetics. But what if he was right that happiness comes from needing less, not having more? What if our whole approach to solving homelessness is wrong because we're trying to fit people into an economic system that's fundamentally broken?"

Jon looked out at the crowd, which was growing larger as the start time approached. "So you think this whole rally is pointless?"

"Not pointless. But maybe incomplete." Amanda stood up, smoothing down her jacket. "Gandhi used to fast---not as a hunger strike, but as a way to purify his own intentions while appealing to other people's conscience. Sometimes I wonder if those of us organizing these events should be asking what we're willing to sacrifice, not just what we're demanding from others."

"That sounds like victim-blaming," Jon said, his tone sharpening. "Like suggesting that if poor people just had better attitudes or made better choices, they wouldn't be homeless."

"No, I mean us," Amanda clarified. "What are we willing to sacrifice? Our comfort, our convenience, our assumptions about how the world should work? Gandhi would probably look at our housing crisis and say that it's not really about scarcity---it's about how we've organized ourselves around the idea that some people deserve security and others don't."

Jon stood up as well, checking his watch. "I still think you're being too idealistic. We need concrete policy changes, not philosophical transformation."

"But what if those things aren't separate?" Amanda asked. "Gandhi always said that the means are as important as the ends. If we're trying to create a more just society through methods that maintain the same power dynamics---us speaking for them, us deciding what they need---then maybe we're not actually creating justice."

"Alright," Jon said, "but what would that look like practically? How do we organize differently?"

Amanda paused, watching Sarah approach their group hesitantly, carrying a sign she'd made herself. "Maybe we start by admitting that the people experiencing homelessness understand their situation better than we do. Maybe instead of organizing a rally about them, we organize with them. Maybe we stop and really listen when they tell us that sometimes the shelters are more dangerous than the streets, or that the 'services' we're so proud of are humiliating to access."

"That's harder to coordinate," Jon pointed out.

"Yeah, it is. But Gandhi would probably say that anything worth doing is hard. He spent decades learning that you can't transform society without transforming yourself, that you can't love people from a distance, that real change requires you to see your opponents as teachers instead of enemies."

"Opponents as teachers?"

"Like the city council members who vote against housing funding," Amanda explained. "Instead of just calling them heartless, what if we tried to understand what they're afraid of? What if we approached them with curiosity instead of just anger?"

Jon looked skeptical. "Some of them genuinely don't care about poor people."

"Maybe. But Gandhi would probably say that our job isn't to judge their hearts---it's to appeal to whatever capacity for compassion they have while making sure our own hearts stay open." Amanda gestured toward the gathering crowd. "Look at all this energy, all this passion. But how much of it is driven by love for our neighbors, and how much is driven by anger at our opponents?"

"Anger can be motivating," Jon said.

"Sure, but it can also be corrupting. Gandhi used to say that hatred can't drive out hatred, only love can do that. Not sentimental love, but the kind of love that's willing to suffer for truth rather than make others suffer."

Jon was quiet for several moments. Finally, he said, "So if Gandhi were here today, you think he'd tell us to call off the rally?"

"No," Amanda said thoughtfully. "But I think he'd ask us to be really honest about our motivations. Are we here because we want to feel good about ourselves, or because we're genuinely committed to serving the poorest people in our community? Are we demanding that others change while we stay comfortable, or are we willing to experiment with living differently ourselves?"

A volunteer approached them with a question about the microphone setup, and they walked toward the small stage together. As they did, Amanda noticed Sarah talking animatedly with a group of college students, sharing her story, no longer invisible.

"You know what?" Jon said as they reached the stage. "Maybe after today, we should spend more time just listening. Not planning the next event, not strategizing, just sitting with people and learning from them."

"Gandhi would probably say that's the most important work of all," Amanda replied. "Understanding that we're all connected, that someone else's suffering diminishes all of us, that real solutions have to honor everyone's dignity."

The crowd was fully assembled now, voices rising in conversation and anticipation. But as Amanda looked out at the faces---housed and unhoused, young and old, angry and hopeful---she found herself thinking less about the speeches they were about to give and more about the conversations they needed to have afterward. The long, difficult, transformative work of building relationships across difference, of questioning their own assumptions, of discovering what it might mean to truly serve rather than simply advocate.

Gandhi would probably say that was where the real change would begin.

John Coltrane

John Coltrane was an American jazz saxophonist and composer who revolutionized modern jazz through his innovative improvisational techniques and spiritual approach to music, becoming one of the most influential musicians of the 20th century through his work with Miles Davis and his own legendary quartet, culminating in masterpieces like "A Love Supreme" before his death from liver cancer at age 40.

The Sound of Understanding

The late afternoon sun streamed through the tall windows of the New York Jazz Festival office as Ashley knocked twice on the mahogany door before entering. Behind her, her sixteen-year-old son Ben shuffled in, earbuds dangling around his neck, his attention split between his phone and the unfamiliar surroundings.

"Ashley! Perfect timing," called Tommy, the festival director, looking up from a scattered array of schedules and vendor contracts spread across his desk. Two young women sat in chairs near the window, laptops open. "And you must be Ben. Your mother's told me so much about you."

"Taylor, Nicole—this is Ashley, our operations manager, and her son Ben," Tommy said, gesturing toward the women. Taylor, who appeared to be in her mid-twenties with dark curly hair, looked up and smiled warmly. Nicole, slightly older with glasses and a vibrant scarf, gave a friendly wave.

"We're just going over the digital marketing strategy for the festival," Taylor explained, closing her laptop slightly.

Ben offered a polite nod while Ashley set her briefcase down and pulled out a thick folder. "I've got the final vendor confirmations and the security logistics you requested. Everything should be set for next week."

Tommy leaned back in his chair, a satisfied smile crossing his weathered face. "Excellent. You know, I've been thinking about the atmosphere we want to create as people arrive each day. I want something that immediately tells them they're entering sacred musical territory."

"What did you have in mind?" Ashley asked, settling into the chair across from his desk while Ben wandered over to examine the framed photographs of jazz legends lining the walls.

"John Coltrane's recording of 'My Favorite Things,'" Tommy said without hesitation. "We'll have it playing softly throughout the festival grounds as the crowds filter in. There's something about that piece—the way it builds, the spiritual searching in every note. It'll set exactly the right mood."

Nicole perked up. "Oh, that's brilliant. We can work that into the social media campaign—maybe share some of the history behind the piece."

Ben looked up from a black-and-white photograph of a man holding a saxophone. "Who the heck is John Coltrane?"

The silence that followed was so profound that even the ambient noise of New York traffic seemed to pause. Ashley's pen stopped mid-signature. Tommy's coffee cup froze halfway to his lips. Taylor and Nicole exchanged incredulous glances.

"I'm sorry, what did you just say?" Tommy asked slowly, as if he couldn't quite believe what he'd heard.

"Ben!" Ashley exclaimed, her voice a mixture of embarrassment and genuine shock. "How do you not know who John Coltrane is?"

The teenager shrugged, unfazed by their reactions. "I mean, I listen to music. I just don't know... old music, I guess?"

Taylor set her laptop aside and stood up. "Wait, seriously? You've never heard of Coltrane?"

"This is a crisis," Nicole added, shaking her head with a slight smile. "An actual educational emergency."

Tommy set down his coffee and stood up, walking over to where Ben stood near the photographs. "Son, this isn't just 'old music.' This is John Coltrane—arguably one of the most important musicians who ever lived. What you're looking at right there," he pointed to the photograph Ben had been examining, "is a man who changed not just jazz, but the entire landscape of American music."

Ashley shook her head in disbelief. "Ben, I can't believe I never... we need to fix this right now."

For the next twenty minutes, the office became an impromptu classroom. Tommy pulled out vinyl records while Ashley searched for videos on her tablet. Taylor pulled up streaming playlists on her phone, and Nicole began sharing fascinating articles she'd bookmarked about Coltrane's legacy.

"See, the thing about Coltrane," Tommy explained, carefully placing a worn copy of "A Love Supreme" on his turntable, "is that he understood something most musicians never grasp. For him, music wasn't entertainment or even art in the traditional sense—it was prayer. Every time he picked up his saxophone, he was communing with something greater than himself."

Ben listened as the opening notes filled the room. "It sounds... intense. Like he's trying to say something really important."

"Exactly!" Ashley said, her earlier embarrassment replaced by enthusiasm. "Coltrane believed that music could transform people, that it could connect them to the divine spark within themselves. He wasn't just playing notes—he was channeling something deeper."

Taylor moved closer, her eyes bright with passion. "I grew up listening to Coltrane because of my grandfather. He always said that Coltrane's music saved him during some of his darkest times. There's this transcendent quality to it that's hard to explain until you really listen."

Tommy nodded, his eyes closed as he listened to the familiar melody. "He once said that the highest purpose of creative expression is to offer a gift of transformation to everyone who listens with an open heart. That's why 'My Favorite Things' is perfect for the festival opening. It starts with something familiar—a song from 'The Sound of Music'—but then takes you on this incredible journey of discovery."

"But why that song specifically?" Ben asked, his earlier disinterest replaced by genuine curiosity.

"Because Coltrane and his quartet—McCoy Tyner on piano, Elvin Jones on drums, and Jimmy Garrison on bass—they'd play it for thirty minutes or more," Ashley explained, having absorbed countless conversations with Tommy over the years. "Not to show off, but because the music kept revealing new truths. They called it collective improvisation, but Coltrane thought of it as group prayer."

Nicole adjusted her glasses and leaned forward. "What's fascinating is how he approached his instrument. He practiced for hours every day, even at the height of his fame. There are stories about him falling asleep with his saxophone in his hands. That level of dedication is inspiring no matter what field you're in."

Tommy walked back to his desk and picked up another album. "Here's what made him special, Ben. He never stopped learning, never stopped practicing, but he understood that real practice went beyond just technical exercises. He studied Indian music, African rhythms, modal structures. He was willing to follow his curiosity even when critics didn't understand what he was doing."

"People actually criticized him?" Ben asked, surprised.

"Oh, absolutely," Tommy laughed. "When he started exploring what they called 'free jazz,' when he began those long, searching solos, some critics called him self-indulgent. But Coltrane was following an inner voice that demanded complete expression. He trusted the journey the music was taking him on."

Taylor nodded enthusiastically. "That's what we try to communicate in our marketing—that jazz isn't some stuffy, untouchable thing. It's about exploration and risk-taking. Coltrane embodied that spirit completely."

Ashley leaned forward in her chair. "And that's something you could learn from, Ben. Coltrane learned from masters like Miles Davis and Dizzy Gillespie, but eventually he had to step away and discover what John Coltrane had to say, not what others expected him to say."

"Miles Davis actually fired him once," Tommy added. "In 1957, because of Coltrane's heroin addiction. It hurt him deeply, but it forced him to confront who he really was and who he wanted to become. That same year, he had what he called a spiritual awakening that changed everything."

Ben was quiet for a moment, processing. "So he was struggling with drugs?"

"He was," Ashley said gently. "And he never tried to hide from that. He embraced the struggle as part of his path. He believed that facing difficulty with presence and courage leads to greater music than running from it ever could. Every challenge, every setback—it all became part of his spiritual and artistic development."

Nicole spoke up softly. "My sister went through addiction recovery, and she told me that Coltrane's story gave her hope. The idea that you can transform your pain into something beautiful, something that helps others—that's powerful."

"Exactly," Tommy said. "And that's the legacy he left. Not just incredible music, but a roadmap for how to live with purpose and integrity."

Tommy returned to the turntable and carefully lifted the needle. "Here's what I want you to understand, Ben. Coltrane didn't separate his spiritual seeking from his artistic excellence—for him, they were the same path. The deeper he went into his craft, the more he touched something universal. The more honestly he expressed his soul, the more he spoke to the souls of others."

"That's beautiful," Ben said quietly, and all four adults could see that something had shifted in his understanding.

"You know what his biggest regret was?" Ashley asked. "Not the struggle itself, but the time that addiction stole from his development as both a musician and a human being. Those years in the early fifties when he was unreliable, when he disappointed people who believed in him. He never stopped wishing he'd understood earlier that music was his path to something greater."

Taylor pulled out her phone. "Hey, I'm creating a playlist for you right now. Start with 'A Love Supreme,' then 'Giant Steps,' then 'My Favorite Things.' Promise me you'll listen with good headphones, no distractions."

"I promise," Ben said, and he meant it.

Tommy smiled, watching the transformation in the young man's face. "When you hear 'My Favorite Things' next week as you walk through the festival gates, I want you to remember this conversation. Remember that you're about to enter a space where people gathered to experience that same thing Coltrane was searching for—that connection to something infinite through sound."

Ben nodded slowly, then looked up at everyone in the room with new respect. "Can I... can I listen to more of his music? I mean, really listen?"

Ashley, Tommy, Taylor, and Nicole exchanged meaningful glances.

"Son," Tommy said, walking over to his extensive record collection, "I think John Coltrane would tell you to keep searching, keep practicing, keep praying through whatever art speaks to your soul. He'd say the music will lead you home—if you're brave enough to follow where it wants to take you."

Nicole stood and gathered her laptop. "And if you want to talk about what you hear, we're always here. That's what jazz is all about—community and conversation."

"We're planning a pre-festival listening party," Taylor added. "You should come. We'll dive deeper into the artists performing, including a whole session on Coltrane's influence on modern jazz."

As they gathered their things to leave, Ben took one last look at the photograph of Coltrane, seeing not just an old musician, but a seeker who had transformed struggle into transcendence, questions into prayers, and silence into the most profound music ever created.

The sound of understanding had finally begun.

Howard R. Hughes, Jr.

Howard Hughes was an American aviator, filmmaker, and business magnate who became one of the world's wealthiest individuals through his inherited Hughes Tool Company fortune, achieved fame for setting aviation speed records and producing groundbreaking films like "Hell's Angels," transformed Las Vegas through massive casino investments, and spent his final decades as an increasingly reclusive figure plagued by obsessive-compulsive disorder and chronic pain from a near-fatal 1946 plane crash.

The Price of Perfection

The October sun slanted through the stained glass windows of Limestone Baptist Church, casting colored shadows across the fellowship hall as the congregation filtered in after Sunday service. Pastor Mike adjusted his tie and surveyed the modest gathering---about twenty-five folks, mostly seniors, settling into folding chairs arranged in a loose circle. The smell of fresh coffee and Miss Taylor's famous pound cake filled the air.

"Well now, looks like we got some new faces today," Pastor Mike announced with his warm Alabama drawl. "Let's go around and introduce ourselves, shall we?"

An elderly man with silver hair and twinkling eyes raised his hand. "I'm Pat, just moved here from Birmingham to be closer to my granddaughter. Been attending First Baptist there for, oh, forty-some years."

"Welcome, Pat!" Pastor Mike shook his hand firmly. "What brings you our way, besides family?"

Pat chuckled. "Well, Pastor, I figured it was time to slow down a bit. I've been what you might call a movie man for the past thirty years."

"Oh, an actor?" asked Kathy, leaning forward with interest.

"Not exactly," Pat grinned. "More like a professional background person. An extra, you might say. If there was a movie filming anywhere within driving distance, I'd show up. Not for the money---Lord knows they don't pay extras much---but for the glamour of it all. Being part of something bigger, you know?"

Pastor Mike nodded thoughtfully. "That sounds fascinating. What was your favorite picture to work on?"

"Well now, that's easy," Pat's eyes lit up. "My last one, actually. A movie called 'The Aviator,' all about this fellow Howard Hughes. Ever hear of him, Pastor?"

Pastor Mike scratched his chin. "The name sounds familiar, but I can't say I know much about him."

"Oh my," Pat settled back in his chair as Miss Taylor handed him a cup of coffee. "Well, after working on that picture, I got so curious about the man that I spent months reading everything I could find. What a story! What a life!"

As the other conversations died down, the group found themselves drawn into Pat's animated telling.

"See, Howard Hughes wasn't just rich---though Lord knows he was that. His daddy invented some kind of drill bit for oil wells back in 1909, and that built the family fortune. But

Howard, he took that money and did things with it that nobody thought possible."

Pat took a sip of coffee and continued. "When he was just twenty-five years old, he decided to make a movie about World War I pilots. Called it 'Hell's Angels.' Everybody in Hollywood told him it couldn't be done---the aerial scenes were too dangerous, too expensive. But Hughes, he spent over three million dollars on it. Three million! In 1930! He crashed real airplanes, fired directors, even switched from silent picture to talking picture right in the middle of production."

"My goodness," whispered Kathy.

"But that was just the beginning," Pat warmed to his subject. "This man didn't just make movies---he set world records flying airplanes. In 1935, he flew this plane he designed himself, the H-1 Racer, and broke the world speed record at 352 miles per hour. Then in 1938, he flew around the entire world in less than four days, cutting the previous record clean in half."

Pastor Mike leaned forward. "Sounds like quite the ambitious fellow."

"Oh, you don't know the half of it. During the war, when the government said it was impossible to build a massive seaplane to transport troops, Hughes went ahead and built one anyway. The press called it the 'Spruce Goose'---had a wingspan longer than a football field. It only flew once, but by golly, it flew."

The room was quiet except for the gentle clink of coffee cups.

"But here's the thing," Pat's voice grew more thoughtful. "After watching that movie and reading about his life, I started thinking about what kind of advice a man like that might give to folks like us. You know, about living a productive life, making something of ourselves."

"Do tell," Pastor Mike encouraged.

Pat set down his coffee cup. "Well, first thing Hughes would probably say is don't let other people tell you what's impossible. When everyone said he couldn't make 'Hell's Angels,' he made it anyway. When they said you can't fly around the world in four days, he did it in three and three-quarters. The man seemed to believe that if you could envision something, really see it in your mind, then you could make it happen with enough determination."

Kathy nodded slowly. "Sounds a bit like faith, doesn't it?"

"It does indeed," Pat agreed. "And I think he'd say that if you're blessed with success---whether that's money or influence or just respect in your community---you've got a responsibility to use it for something bigger than yourself. Hughes bought up half of Las Vegas back in the sixties, but he wasn't just collecting property. He was giving that whole city legitimacy, employing thousands of people."

"That's a fine principle," Pastor Mike mused.

"But here's where it gets interesting," Pat continued, his voice growing more serious. "Hughes would probably tell us to surround ourselves with excellent people and never settle for second-best in anything we do. His airplane company didn't just build planes---they built planes that pushed the boundaries of what anyone thought aircraft could do. Everything had to be perfect."

He paused, then shook his head sadly. "But I think he'd also warn us about something. See, Hughes got so focused on perfection that sometimes he never finished things at all. He'd spend years and years making a movie or designing an airplane because he wanted everything to be absolutely perfect. And that perfectionism, well, it can become a trap."

The room was very quiet now.

"Most important of all," Pat's voice grew soft, "I think Howard Hughes would tell us never to let success cut us off from the people who matter. In his early days in Hollywood, he had friends---actresses and directors and fellow dreamers. He had connections that made life meaningful."

"What happened to those connections?" Pastor Mike asked gently.

Pat sighed deeply. "Well, that's the tragedy of it all. In 1946, Hughes decided to test-fly one of his experimental aircraft himself. He crashed in Beverly Hills, nearly died, broke just about every bone in his body. The pain was so terrible that he had to take morphine, and that medicine... well, it changed him. He became more and more isolated, more suspicious of people, more alone."

The fellowship hall was utterly silent now.

"As the years went on, Hughes pulled further and further away from the world. He lived in hotel rooms with the curtains drawn, wouldn't let anyone near him, stopped trusting people.

By the time he died in 1976, he was completely alone---one of the richest, most accomplished men in the world, but he had no one left to share it with."

Pat looked around the circle at the faces gathered there. "So I reckon Hughes would tell us to build our dreams, chase what seems impossible, but never---never---let that pursuit cut us off from fellowship like this. Because what good is building an empire if you end up ruling it all by yourself?"

Pastor Mike was quiet for a long moment, then spoke softly. "That's quite a story, Pat. And quite a lesson. Sounds like Mr. Hughes learned some important truths about life, even if he learned them too late to fully benefit from them himself."

"Yes sir," Pat nodded. "The man could envision flying machines that defied gravity, but somehow he couldn't see his way back to the simple human connections that make life worth living."

As the afternoon sun continued to stream through the windows, the group sat in contemplative silence, each perhaps thinking about their own dreams and the people who made those dreams meaningful. In that small Baptist church in northern Alabama, Howard Hughes's hard-won wisdom had found its way into a circle of friends, a gift from a lonely genius to those who still had time to heed his warning.

"Well," Pastor Mike finally said, rising to refill his coffee cup, "I'd say that's about the best Sunday school lesson I've heard in quite some time."

Henry Ford

Henry Ford was an American industrialist and founder of Ford Motor Company who revolutionized manufacturing through assembly line production and made automobiles affordable for ordinary Americans with the Model T, while also pioneering worker-friendly policies like the $5-a-day wage that transformed both the automotive industry and American society.

Workshop Wisdom

Megan pulled her tablet from her bag as she entered the cluttered garage workshop, stepping carefully around half-assembled engine parts and vintage tools. Her mentor, Pete, looked up from the carburetor he was rebuilding, wiping his hands on an oil-stained rag.

"You look frustrated," Pete observed, noting her expression.

"My startup's investors are pushing me to rush our prototype to market," Megan said, settling onto a worn wooden stool. "They want to cut corners on quality to beat our competitors."

Pete nodded thoughtfully. "You know, that reminds me of something Henry Ford faced over a century ago. He went through the same struggle."

"Ford? The car guy?"

"The very one. He actually failed twice before Ford Motor Company succeeded -- the Detroit Automobile Company in 1899, then the Henry Ford Company in 1901. Both times, investors wanted quick profits over his vision of quality."

Megan leaned forward. "What did he do?"

"He started over. In 1903, he found investors who believed in his vision: building a reliable automobile that ordinary working people could afford, not just the wealthy. Everyone told him there was no market for it."

"Sounds familiar," Megan muttered.

Pete picked up a wrench, turning it over in his hands. "Ford had this saying: 'If I had asked people what they wanted, they would have said faster horses.' He understood that real innovation means seeing what people need before they know they need it."

"But how did he convince anyone to take that risk?"

"He proved it through systematic innovation. The assembly line wasn't just about speed -- it was about making quality products affordable. When he introduced the Model T in 1908, he demonstrated that mass demand existed for well-built products at reasonable prices."

Megan pulled up notes on her tablet. "My investors think I'm being too idealistic about worker conditions and fair wages."

Pete's eyes lit up. "Now that's where Ford was truly ahead of his time. In 1914, he introduced the five-dollar, eight-hour workday -- doubling the prevailing wage while reducing hours. People called him crazy."

"Why did he do it?"

"He understood something revolutionary: well-paid workers become customers for the products they build. It created what he called a 'virtuous cycle of prosperity.' His workers could actually afford to buy the cars they were making."

Megan typed notes rapidly. "That's brilliant. Treat your employees well, and they become your market."

"Exactly. Ford believed the greatest innovations should improve life for everyone, not just the innovators." Pete paused, his expression growing more serious. "Of course, Ford was a complex figure. He made significant mistakes -- particularly his promotion of antisemitic views through his newspaper. He later acknowledged the harm this caused, but it reminds us that even visionary leaders can have serious blind spots."

Megan looked up from her tablet. "How do we learn from the good while avoiding the bad?"

"I think Ford himself would say: stay curious, persist through failures, focus on serving real human needs, and remember that with influence comes responsibility. He started as a farm boy who took apart a watch at twelve just to understand how it worked. That curiosity drove everything good that followed."

Pete set down the wrench and looked directly at Megan. "If Ford were advising you today, I think he'd say: trust your instincts about what people truly need, don't be afraid to start over when your vision exceeds what others understand, and build something that makes the world better. Revolutionary change comes from systematically improving processes, not just rushing products to market."

Megan closed her tablet and stood up. "So I should stick to my principles about quality and fair treatment?"

"Ford would probably remind you that success brings the responsibility to lift others up. When his Rouge River plant became the world's largest integrated manufacturing complex, it supported entire communities. Real success isn't just what you accumulate -- it's what you contribute to human progress."

As Megan headed for the door, Pete called after her. "And remember -- Edison himself encouraged Ford when his early companies were struggling. Sometimes you need to prove your capabilities in unexpected ways before the world recognizes your true calling."

Megan smiled. "Thanks, Pete. I think I know what to tell my investors."

"Good luck. And remember -- determined experimentation matters more than prestigious credentials. Ford had minimal formal education, but he changed the world through curiosity and persistence."

As Megan drove away, she thought about Ford's journey from farm boy to industrial revolutionary, and how his best insights about innovation, fairness, and human dignity remained as relevant as ever -- even as his story served as a reminder that great achievements and serious flaws could coexist in the same person, making the lessons both more valuable and more cautionary.

John Wayne

John Wayne was an American film actor who became an enduring cultural icon through his starring roles in over 170 Western and war films, embodying rugged American masculinity and frontier values while winning an Academy Award for "True Grit" and becoming one of Hollywood's most popular and politically influential stars during the mid-20th century.

Leave the Campfire Brighter

The conversation started innocently enough. Michael and Missy were killing time in the hotel bar after a long day at the sales conference, scrolling through their phones when Missy stumbled across an old Western on the TV mounted above the bartender.

"God, they don't make movie stars like that anymore," Missy said, nodding toward the screen where John Wayne was squaring off against some outlaws in what looked like a 1950s Western.

"John Wayne, right?" Michael looked up from his beer. "Yeah, he was before my time, but my dad loved those movies."

Missy's eyes lit up with the kind of enthusiasm that meant Michael was in for a lecture. She'd been in Hollywood for fifteen years as a talent agent, and her knowledge of film history was encyclopedic—and something she loved to share.

"You know what I find fascinating about the Duke?" Missy said, settling back in her chair. "It's not just that he was this iconic tough guy on screen. From everything I've read about him, heard from people who worked with him, the man had this incredible philosophy about life that he lived by. Real practical wisdom."

Michael raised an eyebrow. "Like what?"

"Well, take his whole approach to adversity," Missy continued, warming to her subject. "Wayne would probably tell you that you never let circumstances define your character—you let your character define how you respond to circumstances. He lived that. Did you know he lost his football scholarship at USC because of a bodysurfing accident? Could have given up, felt sorry for himself. Instead, he took whatever work he could get at the studios, starting as a prop man. That's how he met John Ford, which changed everything."

"Huh." Michael found himself genuinely interested despite Missy's tendency toward monologues. "So he'd be one of those 'everything happens for a reason' guys?"

"More like 'everything happens, period—what matters is what you do about it,'" Missy replied. "And he was huge on treating people with respect, regardless of their position. When he was starting out, doing extra work and hauling props, he made it a point to learn everyone's name—from the studio executives down to the guy sweeping the sound stage. He understood that every person contributes to making the magic happen."

Missy paused to take a sip of her wine, but Michael could tell she was just getting started.

"You know what Wayne would tell someone like you, in sales?" she continued. "Find mentors and listen to them, but don't lose yourself trying to please everyone. John Ford was his mentor—tough as nails, demanding—but Ford pushed him to become better. Wayne said Ford taught him the difference between inhabiting a character and just playing yourself in different clothes."

"That's actually pretty good advice," Michael admitted. "Though I bet it was easier to stick to your principles when you're John Wayne."

Missy shook her head. "That's where you're wrong. Wayne would say standing up for what you believe in is especially important when it's unpopular. He never hid his political views in Hollywood, even when it cost him. But here's the thing—he also learned there's a difference between standing firm in your principles and being so rigid that you can't listen to other viewpoints or admit when you're wrong."

She gestured toward the screen where Wayne was now in the middle of a saloon brawl. "And he'd tell you to take your work seriously but not take yourself too seriously. Even when he was dealing with heavy themes—courage, honor, justice—he never lost his sense of humor. The joy has to show through, or what's the point?"

Michael was beginning to see why Missy was successful in her field. Her passion was infectious. "Sounds like he had it all figured out."

"Not exactly," Missy said, her voice taking on a more serious tone. "Wayne would be the first to tell you not to let past mistakes keep you from trying to do better. He knew he was wooden as an actor when he started—the critics knew it, audiences knew it. But he kept working at it, kept learning. Took him years to really find his footing."

She paused, looking thoughtful. "And he'd probably tell you that your legacy isn't just what you accomplish professionally, but how you treat the people who depend on you. He was married three times, had seven kids, and by his own admission wasn't always the husband or father he should have been. The work, the travel, the demands of the business—he said those were explanations, not excuses."

Michael found himself nodding. "That hits close to home."

"Here's what I think Wayne would say to anyone today," Missy continued, leaning forward. "Use whatever platform life gives you to make the world a little better. He realized that even playing cowboys and soldiers could serve a purpose—entertainment lifts spirits, stories about courage and integrity inspire people to be their best selves."

She looked back at the TV where the credits were rolling on the Western. "And you know what? If he were sitting here right now, he'd probably tell us both to put down the damn cigarettes—though these days it might be put down the phones, step away from social media, stop poisoning ourselves with things that don't serve us. He'd say life's like making a movie—you get one take to get it right, so make it count."

Michael was quiet for a moment, processing. "You really think about this stuff, don't you?"

Missy smiled. "When you work in this business long enough, you realize the really great ones weren't just talented—they had something to say about how to live. Wayne's advice would be pretty simple: stand tall, speak the truth, treat others with dignity, and leave the campfire a little brighter than you found it."

As if on cue, another Western started playing on the TV. Michael found himself actually paying attention this time, wondering what other wisdom might be hidden behind that familiar drawl and easy confidence.

"Want another round?" he asked. "I'm thinking I could use a few more lessons from the Duke."

Missy grinned. "Now you're talking, pilgrim."

Arthur Miller

Arthur Miller was an American playwright who became one of the most influential dramatists of the 20th century through works like "Death of a Salesman" and "The Crucible," exploring themes of moral responsibility, the American Dream, and social justice while winning the Pulitzer Prize and courageously challenging McCarthyism during the Red Scare era.

Speaking Truth to Power

Sarah stirred her latte absently as she glanced up from her dog-eared copy of *The Crucible*. "I just finished this for my American Literature class. Miller was good, but I don't know... sometimes I feel like his characters are so heavy, you know? Always struggling with these big moral dilemmas."

Landon looked up from his laptop where he'd been grading student papers. As a theater professor, he'd spent decades teaching Miller's works. "Heavy, maybe, but that's exactly what made him brilliant. Miller once said that if he could give advice to writers, the first thing would be to write what troubles you, not just what you know."

"What do you mean by that?"

Landon leaned back in his chair, warming to a subject he was passionate about. "Well, Miller watched his father lose everything in the stock market crash of 1929. That experience of seeing a confident man reduced to confusion and despair— that's what eventually became *Death of a Salesman* twenty years later. Willy Loman wasn't his father, but he carried that same bewilderment at a world that suddenly stopped making sense."

Sarah nodded slowly. "So he was drawing from real life?"

"Absolutely, but here's the key—he'd say you have to transform personal experience through imagination. Don't just write autobiography. Take that emotional truth and shape it into something universal." Landon gestured with his coffee cup. "Like with *All My Sons*. He heard about a real businessman who sold faulty aircraft parts during World War II, causing pilots' deaths. But Miller filtered that through his own questions about moral responsibility and the cost of success."

"I never knew that," Sarah said, genuinely interested now. "But what about *The Crucible*? That was about the Salem witch trials."

Landon smiled. "On the surface, yes. But Miller would tell you never to be afraid to use your platform to speak truth to power, even when it costs you. Everyone understood that play was really about McCarthyism—the communist witch hunts tearing apart Hollywood in the 1950s. The play initially failed on Broadway because audiences weren't ready for such a direct challenge. And when the House Un-American Activities Committee summoned Miller himself, they demanded he name names of people he'd seen at communist gatherings. He refused, was found in contempt of Congress, and faced possible prison time."

"Wow. He really put his money where his mouth was."

"That's exactly what he'd advise any writer—that standing up for principle isn't always popular, but it's necessary if art is to maintain its integrity." Landon paused, then continued. "But here's something else Miller was passionate about: writing about ordinary people with the same seriousness others reserve for kings and generals. When *Death of a Salesman* opened, critics questioned whether a failed salesman's story could carry the weight of classical tragedy. Miller believed dignity isn't the privilege of the highborn—it belongs to anyone willing to fight for their sense of self-worth."

Sarah was taking notes now. "So the traveling salesman, the factory worker—their struggles are just as worthy of serious treatment?"

"Exactly. And Miller understood that all great drama is fundamentally about moral choice under pressure. Whether he was writing about Salem's witch trials or a Brooklyn longshoreman's crisis of conscience in *A View from the Bridge*, he was always asking: what happens when someone must choose between competing loyalties? Between personal survival and moral principle? Between the individual and the community?"

"That's what makes his characters so intense," Sarah realized.

"Right. But Miller would also tell you not to let success insulate you from the struggles that gave your work its power. After *Death of a Salesman* made him wealthy and famous, he had to work consciously to stay connected to the economic anxieties and social pressures that shaped his understanding of American life."

Landon's expression grew more thoughtful. "He'd also emphasize that theater is a collective art form—you have to respect your collaborators. When Elia Kazan directed *Death of a Salesman*, he brought insights to Willy Loman that Miller hadn't fully seen himself. Good directors and actors don't just interpret your words—they complete them."

"That's a pretty humble perspective for such a successful playwright."

"Miller learned to be prepared to defend his work but also willing to learn from criticism. *The Crucible* found new relevance when it was revived in the 1960s—audiences suddenly saw parallels to other forms of political persecution. Sometimes a work needs time to find its proper moment."

Sarah closed her book thoughtfully. "It sounds like he really understood that writing is about more than just craft—it's about moral responsibility."

Landon nodded, his voice becoming quieter. "Miller believed the theater teaches us that the human heart is capable of both profound cruelty and extraordinary grace, sometimes within the same character, sometimes within the same moment. He'd tell writers to write with compassion for human frailty, but never lose your outrage at human callousness. The stage is where we go to see ourselves clearly, in all our complexity and contradiction."

"That's beautiful," Sarah said. "Makes me want to reread *The Crucible* with fresh eyes."

"Miller would have liked that," Landon smiled. "He always said the theater was about truth and conscience—helping us understand what it means to be human in all our messy, complicated glory."

As Sarah packed up her books, she felt she understood something new about why Miller's characters felt so heavy, so real. They carried the weight of genuine moral struggle—the kind that defines who we really are when everything else is stripped away.

Cover Photo Credits

The photographs featured on the cover of this book were sourced under *Creative Commons* licenses, which allow photographers and artists to share their work with specific permissions for reuse and publication. Creative Commons provides a standardized licensing framework that enables creators to grant others the right to use, distribute, and sometimes modify their work while retaining certain rights. The generous photographers whose images appear in these pages have chosen to make their work available through these open licensing agreements, allowing publishers and authors to access high-quality visual content for educational, artistic, and commercial purposes while properly crediting the original creators.

"Coincidences: A Lincoln - JF Kennedy" by dbking

"Steve Jobs Headshot 2010-CROP" by Matthew Yohe (talk)

"Public Domain: Dr. Martin Luther King, jr. at 1963 March on Washington by USIA (NARA)" by pingnews.com

"Vintage President John F. Kennedy Postcard, In Memoriam Of HIs Death,

Published By Silberne Souvenir Sales, Postmarked 1965" by France1978

"Lucille Ball" by austinmini1275

"Walter Cronkite" by Peabody Awards

"Sir Arthur Conan Doyle, 1892" by w_kites

"American Masters: Marilyn Monroe" by 1950sUnlimited

"Margaret Thatcher" by Unknown photographer

"Jackie Robinson, NPG 97 135" by Harry Warnecke / Frank Livia / Robert F. Cranston / William Klein

"Admiraal Chester W. Nimitz, Bestanddeelnr 900-6787" by Anefo

"Thomas Jefferson" by immugmania

"Amelia Earhart - Colorized" by DonkeyHotey

"Albert Einstein - Colorized" by DonkeyHotey

"Mahatma Gandhi" by Debarshi Ray

"Coltrane" by Gelderen, Hugo van / Anefo

"Howard-Hughes-1938" by RockSkater99

"Henry Ford II in Nederland om zijn jacht te bekijken. Hier op Schiphol, Bestanddeelnr 914-9054 (cropped)" by Hugo van Gelderen / Anefo

"John Wayne - still portrait -2" by EatPay3

"Arthur Miller" by Huntington Theatre Company

About the Author

Thomas "Tom" Campbell calls Wilmington, North Carolina home, where he lives alongside his canine companion, Watson. Throughout his varied career, Tom has built expertise across several sectors, notably serving as an Account Executive and Industry Consultant at AT&T Information Systems. His entrepreneurial pursuits have included collaborating with his son Jonathan to run Beach PC, a community-focused computer repair service, while also founding and operating Advanced Legal Software, a statewide enterprise that developed specialized applications for family law practices. This breadth of experience reflects Tom's adaptability and business acumen across both corporate and independent ventures.

Beyond his professional pursuits, Tom maintains an active personal life centered around his community and interests. He is a dedicated member of the Sherlock Holmes Society of the Cape Fear, serves as a Sunday school teacher at the First Baptist Church of Carolina Beach, and treasures time spent on family vacations.